LIFE IN THE UNIVERSE

In memory of my parents

LIFE IN THE UNIVERSE

Stories

Michael J. Farrell

The Stinging Fly

A Stinging Fly Press Book

Life In The Universe is first published simultaneously in paperback
and in a special casebound edition (100 copies) in May 2009.

The Stinging Fly Press
PO Box 6016
Dublin 8
www.stingingfly.org

Set in Palatino
Printed by Betaprint, Dublin

ISBN 978-1-906539-07-8 (clothbound)
978-1-906539-08-5 (paperback)

The excerpt on page 59 from *The Artful Universe Expanded* by John D. Barrow is reprinted with the permission of Oxford University Press.

A version of 'Pascal's Wager' was placed second in the 2006 Francis MacManus Awards and was subsequently broadcast on RTE Radio. The version here was first published in *The Stinging Fly*, which also published 'Gravity'. 'Writer-in-Residence' first appeared in *Let's Be Alone Together* (The Stinging Fly Press, 2008). 'The Writtern Word' was published in *The Faber Book of Best New Irish Short Stories 2006-2007* edited by David Marcus (Faber and Faber, 2007).

 The Stinging Fly Press gratefully acknowledges the financial support of The Arts Council/ An Chomhairle Ealaíon.

Contents

The Rift Valley

Packy Bannon's silhouette rode the silhouette of his bicycle along the horizon. If you had a competition for the slowest cyclist in Ireland, Packy would win by a mile. A sycamore tree inched up to meet him. October winds had stripped the trees until spring. In the distance a small dark cloud tried to sideswipe the sun going down in a hurry.

The sun was a wonder in the mind-bending vault of sky. But so was the bicycle, not to mention the rider, our most complex creation as we entered the third millennium, or the fourth or the fortieth depending on where you started counting. The world has been going around for ten or twenty billion years. It seems a long time until you stop to wonder how so much could get done so soon. A lumpy stone in a field takes time. The human knee must have taken ages. And an average brain would make you proud to be a citizen of Earth, which they say has been here only a couple of billion years, a late arrival among the stars.

A speedy cyclist would not have time to notice any of this.

Besides, slow cyclists might surprise you. Two years before, Packy had dismantled the bike, packed it in a case, and flown west to tour Montana. He never boasted about the sights he saw, such as skyscrapers or life in the fast lane. It was mountainy, he would tell people.

Packy now cycled across the face of the orange sun. The bike slowed further, then stopped. He took binoculars from the saddlebag and aimed them at the strand road, followed the road for a mile. He looked at his outsize watch; she was punctual as a rule.

Beyond the strand road was the strand and beyond that the ocean and then America and if you kept going and finished the gyre you would be back under Ben Bulben. Up the road was Classiebawn, a bleak castle crowned with turrets on a prize stretch of land, where Lord Mountbatten lived on and off until the lads blew him up.

Then, there she was, a speck in the dusk: Dalia moving briskly, a natural walker. Packy returned the binoculars to the saddlebag. The bike gathered speed, took a right on the strand road.

Her little head was high and proud, it was bound to be working overtime, like Packy's. She surely had heard of him. The talk couldn't help reaching her.

'Nice evening now.'

Not a word from her. If he looked he might see a hint of a smile, but he dared not look. If only she would break the rules, get rambunctious and wave and yell some crazy greeting, even in her own tongue, or jump on the back of the bicycle and wrap her little black arms around his waist and even grab his personal possessions and cause a sensation. This was surely the only planet where you'd ride by and say no more than it's a nice evening.

Packy rode on, eyes fixed on the road. When the time was ripe, he would know what to say, and maybe so would she.

His father had been a cobbler. When he retired, Packy cleared the decks and opened a shoe shop. Tongue in cheek, he called the place Bigger & Better Shoes. People jumped to the logical conclusion that he catered only to outsize feet. He had vague plans to remedy this misconception but apathy had a silver lining and, in time, word of mouth spread that Packy's place was your best big-boot bet in the Northwest.

He was neither debonair nor charismatic. He was solid and

personable, qualities he looked down on. He turned bald early, smack on the vulnerable front dome, yet he never tried to cover it up with stray strands borrowed from elsewhere. If one were choosing an emissary to send across Montana on a bike, one might pass over Packy, yet in real life it is people like Packy who go.

In a picturesque town between Ben Bulben and the sea it was natural that The Maeve, a singing pub, would attract locals as well as tourists. Packy drank there, got his pub grub there, played cards and darts and kept an eye out for women. One quiet Saturday night, the cards were interrupted by rowdy members of the Coleman's football club. The team had just lost a semi-final.

'It's better than losing a fucking final,' one of them said. This led to a debate about the relative merits of losing a final or a semi-final.

Then, for no obvious reason, Willie McGinley started telling how a black girl had applied for a job at the garage where he specialised in vans and four-wheel drives. He was known as 'the Kick' McGinley because, on a windy day five years before, he had taken a sideline kick from forty yards out that followed a dream trajectory into the corner of the net. That, too, had been in a semi-final.

Folklore flourishes at peak moments in the life of a community. People talk about big ideas such as destiny. Attention turns like the shivering hand of a compass to certain chosen individuals, in this case McGinley. Such exalted moments are brought about not just by drink but by some deep hankering in the human heart. Songs get written and then sung. But on this occasion there was no time for singing them. In the ensuing final, McGinley broke his leg and the team lost. One could not blame him for arguing that it was better to lose the semi-final.

'You want to see black?' the Kick was saying about the girl. 'So I asked her where she came from. Kenya, says she.'

'Kenya!' a raw youth echoed, fueling the Kick's narrative.

'And did you give her the job, Kick?'

'Do I look like the foreign missions?' the Kick responded. 'The foreign missions,' he repeated as if he had hit on a dandy turn of phrase. 'Let me tell you, those foreign hoors will drive the Irish out of house and home if something isn't done. They're prepared to work for half nothing until they get their foot in the door. Then one morning you wake up and they own your business.'

'You said a mouthful, Kick.'

'Go on out of that, I said to her. I need someone with, how shall I say, sophistication,' the Kick imitated himself telling the girl off.

'It doesn't take a lot of sophistication to keep your books, Kick.'

In the silence, everyone looked around to see who had spoken. Their eyes came to rest on Packy Bannon calmly shuffling the cards.

'What did you say?' said the Kick.

'You heard me.' There was another pregnant pause. 'She might be a good bookkeeper,' Packy said in a conciliatory way.

'Well, listen to him,' the Kick mocked. 'Listen to the hoor.' He looked around at the footballers for support. But the subject was touchy and the atmosphere charged. Foreigners were no problem when they arrived from Lithuania or Poland and settled in Dublin. Now, though, they were branching out everywhere, taking over the computers in the library, double-parking new Toyotas outside Peggie's for Sunday breakfast. Even when they spoke English well, the accent was foreign. Not knowing what was going on in their heads, locals worried. Opinions were quietly formed and became grudges a day at a time. The grudges were kept to a whisper. Someone from Brussels or The Hague might be listening. Or bleeding hearts like Packy.

'She could have done the job, is all I'm saying.' Packy did not know the girl. He had no idea why he had spoken up.

'And how the fuck would you know?'

'Forget about it.'

'I won't forget about it,' McGinley put down his pint and got to his feet. Packy was already dealing another hand of cards. 'I won't forget about it,' the Kick repeated, running out of ideas. 'Come outside and I'll show you what I mean.'

The hand Packy dealt was never played. The invitation to come outside was old as Cain and Abel. Sometimes it was bad communication, sometimes a conflict of interest. Mostly, it was ego. Or honour, as it was called in the so-called age of chivalry. Often it meant war. Packy's mind had little time just then for the great sweep of history. This was a personal crisis calling for decision. It used to be, when they went outside, that pistols were used, or swords—it was a relief to think it wouldn't come to that. But it could still be ugly, even dangerous. Hard to believe how quickly life could change.

'What good would it do, Kick?'

'You started it,' the Kick said. Packy knew McGinley since the national school. When McGinley was six, Packy would have been twelve or thirteen. He should have beaten the shite out of him then, his racing mind mused. He could not recall at what exact age the balance of power changed, the day when the Kick became taller or stronger than himself. After that the chance was gone. Not that it ever mattered, until tonight, and not even tonight—it was only a misunderstanding. 'Or are you a coward?' the Kick was saying.

Now a decision was surely called for. Just as sometimes one got to choose between pleasures, one sometimes had to choose between fears. Fear of the savage McGinley on the one hand and fear of being a coward on the other. He threw the cards on the table in a resigned gesture, as if beating up the Kick were a routine but distasteful duty.

The back yard of The Maeve, surrounded by ramshackle outbuildings, was littered with rusty machinery, plastic bags of farm supplies, generations of bric-a-brac. There were heaps of stones, heaps of sand, and rain puddles in between. There was scarcely room for a fight. The Kick impatiently took off his leather jacket and handed it to one of his followers. Packy considered taking off his own jacket, but decided it would look like more defiance than he actually felt and might spur the Kick to greater fury. He himself was having trouble mustering any real ferocity, but hoped that when the Kick eventually hit him it would do the trick.

Packy surprised everyone, and especially himself, by landing a lucky punch on McGinley that would soon blossom into a black eye. After that it got ugly. The fight was seldom mentioned afterwards, grown men ashamed that they had been party to such a trouncing as Packy received.

Yet Packy Bannon felt no embarrassment at being beaten. He was back playing cards in a couple of days. He wasn't sure what had happened or why. He had stood up for that girl's honour, he told himself, even though he had never met her. In some abstract way he had fought for justice and human dignity. Not that he had taught McGinley any lesson, but he had, he felt, bought back some kind of integrity for the community.

The Kick stopped visiting The Maeve. While he would have preferred to win the fight, Packy found some compensation in thus adjusting McGinley's world.

Dalia got a job in Rose's Flower Shop. Packy would cycle past in the evenings. Just curiosity, he told himself. Lucky woman, when she could have been knee-deep in grease in McGinley's dump. Packy felt vaguely aggrieved that she had never acknowledged how he'd stood up for her. When he met her on the street she did not seem to see him.

As his ribs mended and his own black eye faded to normal, he tried to forget about her. He was planning to cycle around France in the spring along with Jack, one of the card players, who had taken to calling himself Jacques. Each evening Packy cycled farther and faster, getting into shape. He found himself passing Dalia on her way home from Rose's. It dawned on him that some kind of happenstance was kicking in. Well, maybe that was taking it too far: there were several other routes he could take on the bike. But so could she. The bike would slow down to a crawl as Packy wrestled with the metaphysical wrinkles that sometimes creep into the fabric of life. It couldn't be romance. He had scarcely spoken to her. As far as he could see she wasn't much to look at. But then neither was he. And romance wasn't about looks in the long run. He had fought the only fight of his life for this girl. He had a stake in Dalia's future, whatever that might mean—destiny was a crooked road with few signposts.

He decided the shop needed flowers.

'Perhaps roses,' Dalia said.

'It's for a shoe shop,' he said.

'Roses,' she repeated. There was no hint of a smile. Up close she was no prettier than from a distance, but enigmatic, that was it. Some experts suggested the world as we know it started in Kenya. Ancient human remains had been found there and were finally giving up their secrets. Her ancestry might go right back to *homo sapiens*. Her people might have been the first to use stone tools or old pottery. Or poison arrows. There was a hell of a lot of mystery in Kenya. So he bought a few roses every day and stuck them amid the big boots in the shop window.

'I was wondering where in Kenya you came from,' he ventured one day.

'What do you mean?' She was taken aback.

'You're not Maasai, by any chance?' The Kick McGinley had cracked his ribs on account of her, he was entitled to an answer.

'No.'

'And what?'

'Pokot,' she was scarcely audible.

'Never heard of them.'

'I know.'

Cycling past her in the evenings was, he figured, a ritual, a bonding of ancient Kenya with contemporary Ireland. She had a high forehead. The palms of her hands were pink, and he would wonder about other areas. She was popular around town, he noticed. Packy lost interest in rural France and read up on Kenya.

In spring he flew into Nairobi. He cycled up the legendary Rift Valley. When the earth was formed, with desperate erupting and burping, its outer skin ran out of stuffing and left a rift that settled into a valley. Here and there a lake collected water. Round one such lake, a few million years later, many of the world's pink flamingos were congregated, a pink ocean of noise. The hardy Maasai have populated the valley since history began. They are tall and erect and proud, every one a queen or king, oh and black, because the sun is poised over the Rift Valley and there's seldom a cloud for shade.

Eventually Packy came to the Cherangani Hills, and the Elgeyo Escarpment, which drops a mile into the Kerio Valley, home of the Pokot people.

The Kerio Valley stretches to infinity. The clay is burned red and barren because the sun is tireless. The huts are built of rods and clay and cow dung, and the floor is three feet above the ground to keep snakes out of the bed. Ortum is the main town, if you could call it that. If you want a midday meal you'd do better to go down by the river where wiry prospectors are panning the tired water for gold. Down there, for modest money, you could buy a stew from a dirty black skillet, bits of rabbit or snake.

The Pokots are not as tall, nor are they as handsome as the Maasai. The men still carry spears, and not just for photo-ops for tourists, of which there are scarcely any, but because wild animals have not yet surrendered that part of the earth. The women wear beads and bangles, and girls wear white paste on their faces when it comes time to announce they have grown into women.

When Packy returned from safari he mentioned none of this. He only said, as he had said about Montana, it's very mountainy.

His backside was so sore he vowed never to cycle again. He

broke the vow in a week and waited in a drizzle until the speck came walking along the strand road. Off he went after her, head and shoulders leaning into the resisting wind. Her red umbrella defied the elements, held aslant.

'Hello, Dalia,' he said as he drew abreast.

'Hello,' she said in a begrudging voice.

'Everyone in Kenya says hello.'

But she would say no more. She walked on with stoic pride. Pride she may have felt or he may have imagined. He pictured her with the white paste on her face and wondered had she undergone the barbaric rite of circumcision. She could, if she would, tell him about local gods and dancing under the moon, about hair-raising skirmishes involving spears, about witch doctors predicting the outcomes of cattle raids. She was more interesting than anyone Ben Bulben had seen for a century.

She dipped the umbrella, hiding behind it. The prospects for romance were dim. Unless, that is, you focused on the bigger picture, some obscure cosmic roundelay with an unpredictable ending. It wasn't for nothing she'd landed on this old island when there were many other options. And she wasn't made of stone, she no doubt sweated and piddled like anybody else. Her manner could melt. But not this evening, not in this rain. Packy rode on, soaked.

After a month, when local elections were looming, he declared himself a candidate for the county council. He called a news conference and one reporter showed up. He was running as an independent, he told the reporter. His candidacy was about international harmony, he said. The Irish had been pilgrims practically since we left Tír na nÓg. If the Yanks and the Brits had not opened their doors to us when we went into exile, we would have died of misery. Now it was our turn.

'Our turn for what?' the reporter asked him.

'I don't know. Take our place among the nations of the earth, I suppose. If I'm elected to the county council, we'll thrash it out.'

'You have the gift of the gab anyway,' the reporter informed him, glad of potential fireworks in a dull campaign. A picture of Packy and his bike, on a road outside Mombasa, appeared on the front page.

The cards were put aside. The card table in the Maeve became Packy's campaign headquarters, and the card players his staff, five or six raw politicos. Local drinkers flocked around every night, willing him to raise hell.

'Good man yourself, Packy.'

'Jaysus, Packy, you're full of surprises.'

If they had spare change after paying for the drink, they would plonk it on the table as a political contribution.

'But will you vote for me, is the thing?'

'Ah Jaysus, Packy, don't ask me to do that.'

After a week, while Packy and the politicos wrestled with a speech he would give at the church gate on Sunday, the Kick McGinley darkened the door. The pub went quiet, as pubs used to do when John Wayne made his entrance in old westerns.

'And how is yourself, Kick?' the diplomatic barman asked.

Kick shuffled up to the counter and ordered a whiskey and a pint. The lads went back to Packy's speech, which was all about human dignity and how the world would lapse back into chaos unless bigotry were stamped out and replaced by an infusion of mutual respect and, yes, love.

'Maybe love is too strong a word,' one fellow ventured.

'How, too strong?'

'Ah, for fuck's sake, Packy, that kind of talk will get you laughed at.' The bottom had fallen out of the strategy session. The Kick talked quietly to the barman but threw occasional glances in Packy's direction, then frequent ones. This reminded Packy's politicos of errands they had to run, and soon Packy was alone with an empty glass.

'Ye hoor, Packy, can I buy you a drink?' the Kick said from the counter.

'You can if you want.'

'And can I sit down?'

'You can.'

The Kick sat. He held out his hand and they shook. The last time they got this close, it was Armageddon. In the months between they had never spoken. Even in a small town it takes only minor stratagems to steer clear of undesirables. By steering clear, Packy never got a good look at the Kick's black eye. And vice versa.

'You put up a good fight,' the Kick said.

'It's ancient history now.'

'No, it's not. That's what I'm here to talk about. I haven't slept properly from that day to this.' The lounge had gone unnaturally quiet until the Kick looked around and scowled at everyone. The drinkers quickly went back to drinking. 'I did wrong, Packy.'

'I suppose I provoked you.'

'Oh, I don't mean what I did to you. It's that girl I can't get out of my mind,' he said in a confidential tone. 'She's no ordinary girl.'

'How do you know?'

'It must be a sixth sense. I suppose you don't know Aristophanes the Greek?'

'Can't say I do.'

'Aristophanes, if what they say is true, claimed that, back at the beginning, I don't know, before humans, I suppose, there was a primitive crowd, bigger than us—you know?—each of them had four feet and four hands, do you follow me?'

'Sure. Four feet and four hands.'

'They had two faces looking in opposite directions, and all the parts duplicated like that. Are you with me so far?' The Kick, on uncertain ground, told it like it was a foreign language, scratching himself and rubbing his neck and at no time looking the other man in the eye.

'Sure.' Packy raised two fingers for another couple of pints.

'Anyway, these big bastards got, I don't know, uppity, I

suppose. This was in Greece, where the gods took no nonsense from anyone. So Zeus split them in half, down the middle. That left them with two feet and two hands, just like us. Christ, Packy, this is a stupid fucking story, I don't know why I'm telling it. And I'm not even drunk. I just didn't know what to say to you, and I thought this yarn might get me started.'

'Is that the whole story?'

'More or less.' He took a slug from the glass. He looked around to ensure the other customers were minding their own business. Packy's spineless politicos had trickled back into the pub, dumbfounded by developments. Their natural milieu was cards, Packy realised, they were not cut out for shaping the contours of history. The Kick, meanwhile, was breathing heavily, caught between embarrassment and other emotions that had been percolating since Dalia entered his life. 'The thing is: since that day, every human creature is only half a person. So what we're doing, according to Aristophanes—we're searching for our other half.'

Packy feared the Kick would cry. The emotion in his eyes was ready to turn to tears. All at once he knew that McGinley's legendary sideline kick had been a fluke. No longer mythical, he could try for a lifetime without repeating it. He was no savage fighter either, just an ordinary fellow with a sentimental side. If I knew then what I know now, Packy speculated, I would have brought more ferocity of my own to that fight, more myth and less fear, and maybe turned the tables and beaten the tar out of him.

'That's the purpose of love,' the Kick was saying. 'To reunite our severed selves and make us right again. And I don't know why the fuck I'm telling you this.'

'It's a great story, Kick.'

'Not just a story, Packy. It's the way things are.'

'What do you mean?'

'I don't know exactly. But I'm full of regret I didn't hire that girl.'

'She was lucky to escape you,' Packy prepared to duck if the Kick started another fracas. Aristophanes knew a thing or two. Even back then, if you didn't watch out, your heart would cut your throat. Packy felt himself bonding with McGinley in some illogical way that put the fear of God in him. The Kick, too, yearned for Dalia. Though neither of them knew her. She couldn't possibly be the other, missing half of both of them. If it came to a showdown for her hand, though, Packy was confident he would put up a better fight the next time.

'So how's the old campaign going?'

'Going grand.'

'Ye hoor, you're a gas man. Could you use a volunteer?'

'For what?'

'I thought maybe you could use a campaign manager?'

'I have one,' Packy nodded in the direction of a youth drinking lemonade who had no idea he had been elevated to such high office. Packy was worried that McGinley, if he became manager, might sabotage his campaign and, as they said in the movies, get the girl.

'I only wanted to help,' the Kick said, crestfallen.

Two days later, the sun still high in the sky, they cycled along a country road. McGinley had offered the four-wheel drive, but Packy declined. In a four-wheel drive it would look like the Kick was running for office. The strategy was three townlands every evening; that way they would cover the entire constituency by polling day.

'You should see the roads in Kenya,' Packy beat around the bush. 'The potholes are so big the cars have to hoot the horn coming out of them.'

'Did you meet her people?' the Kick asked over a pint back at The Maeve.

'I did not.'

'I hear they're all chiefs and princes. That would make the women blue-blooded as well. I hear the wealth comes from gold mines and oil wells and all. Did you notice anything like that?'

'Didn't notice that at all.'

'Pokots, isn't it?'

'You've done your homework, Kick.'

'I even went into that shop and bought flowers. I apologised for not giving her the job, I might as well tell you. She was polite, but I couldn't get a word out of her.'

'Are you in love with her or something?'

'I am not.' The Kick paused for a slug of beer. 'But I can't get her out of my mind. Do you think is that love, Packy?'

'I don't know. I don't know at all.' Packy didn't mention that he couldn't get her out of his own mind, either. The card-playing politicos wandered into the lounge, ordered drinks at the counter, nodded stiffly to Packy and the Kick at the card table. A political shift was taking place in the community. He might be gaining votes from the football crowd while losing the card-playing population.

'There's no gold, Kick,' Packy said quietly. 'There are no princes, either.' It was only fair to tell McGinley the truth. 'They're a small tribe, maybe a quarter of a million of them. They're divided into the cattle people and the corn people. And there are no gold people.'

'Is that a fact?'

'They're nomads.'

'Nomads, is it?'

'You're better off knowing.'

'Still, she walks like nobility.'

'They wander a huge territory, beyond the Cherangani Hills, red clay as far as the eye can see, and no water, so they have to keep moving.'

'And tell me, Packy, is that why you ran for the county council?'

'Is what why I ran?'

'I don't know. Dalia and that.'

'I'm not sure myself.'

It would be preposterous to say the election was about Dalia.

The other politicians said it was about the usual concerns, such as a new school and fixing the roads for tourists. The immigration issue never surfaced. Outside churches on Sundays, Packy talked about creating the best life ever imagined, a more humane planet long on idealism though short on specifics.

On election day, instead of voting, he took off on the bike. It seemed redundant to vote for himself, illogical to vote for anyone else. He cycled slowly, seeing the world.

Self-Portrait

The only thing worse than night is day. Night is when people usually die, and the only thing worse is to wake up in the morning. If he could have one last wish, he would go in the small hours without knowing it. In this hope he always says goodbye to the world before bed. But in no time at all a new sun is shining on the twelve-year-old calendar, the speckled cat is looking in spitefully from the window sill, while the entrepreneur downstairs puts out the ice cream sign with the greatest possible clatter. Once more Fogarty is condemned to life.

His digs above the ice cream parlour comprise a bedroom, a kitchen, a sitting-room, a library, a studio, a museum, all devoid of boundaries in one poky kingdom no larger than a large loo. But no loo. The toilet is at the top of the stairs. He shares it with customers from downstairs, the dregs of the neighbourhood. One boisterous night, years ago, he confronted half a dozen of them, who then beat him so badly he spent months in the hospital. His body, in several respects, has never been the same. Neither has his mind.

Fogarty plugs in the kettle. He splashes water sparingly on his face, which looks sixty or more and is surrounded by a white beard he cuts back twice a year. Blue corduroy trousers and a wine-red corduroy jacket have been waiting on the dusty floor since last night. There is also a tie on the floor, brownish. It awaits some special occasion.

'Go ahead. Ignore me.' The aggrieved voice sounds suspiciously like his own. It comes from a painting on an easel in the studio surrounded by books and junk.

'Not now,' Fogarty says. Still, he looks at the portrait, which bears his likeness, though this has long been a matter of dispute between them. He calls it Foggy, after himself.

Observers might well look askance at a grumpy, smelly old duffer talking to a picture—if the picture had not spoken first. This scenario is one more example of the astonishing matters that go on behind closed doors.

'That was cute,' Foggy says. 'The black eye.'

Fogarty stirs the instant coffee, steps closer to the picture, peers. No denying it, this is a bad black eye. 'Stop whining. I'll fix it.'

He takes refuge in the past. I grew up happy. I was the smartest kid I knew, scholarships and the lot. I could curl a football and score goals to give you goose bumps. I could talk to jackdaws and sheep and badgers without ever being misunderstood. I could lure little girls into being naughty before any of us knew why. I could sing and dance and jump over the moon. I was loved by my parents and God until the latter pulled the carpet from under everything. This is what he tells himself in tight corners—his birthright.

'You're forgetting something,' Foggy sneers. 'About you being the artist.'

'I was an artist until I ran into you,' Fogarty says to the picture, which is twenty-four inches high by thirty-six inches wide, a sturdy board on a smeared and wobbly easel. The figure is to the left, as if he has just walked into the frame, if it had a frame. Thus the self-portrait, if that's what it is, leaves space for all manner of existence, the world. At this moment there is a spinning sky in which sinister birds hover over yellow fields because Foggy insisted on a background just like Van Gogh's 'Crows over Cornfield.' Fogarty, in a huff, painted tired old crows who wouldn't last the winter.

'I'd actually prefer an Italian background,' the picture had complained. 'Me walking in, oh I don't know, Umbria or that, rolling hills and grapevines from the Renaissance.' Foggy could sound quite grand at times, for a painting. 'But you're not ready for Italy, are you?'

'I'm ready when you are.' That was when Fogarty gave the portrait the black eye.

'You should have gone to art school,' the picture then taunted. Artists who went to art school were forever telling artists who didn't that they should have. But his mother just told him he was an artist, then his teacher told him and his uncle gave him sixpence, and the neighbours dropped in to see his abstract landscapes, a genre no one had tried before. The woman next door asked him to paint her daughter. That picture launched him, back when civilisation was running smoothly. He painted cute girls and fat women and hardy lads. Sometimes he painted birds faintly in the background, on bare branches or dodging clouds, because already the crows were gathering in his head.

'Then you fell plop from your high horse,' the picture can read his mind. This hurts profoundly so that the world beats tin cans and louts shout and bombs go ka-boom and humpty-dumpty has to cling to the wall to avoid becoming a fried egg.

An unseemly number of people he painted died. Not everyone. And not right away. Still in his prime, he wrestled with the law of averages. He talked to shrinks and other experts. He even talked to artists who had gone to art school. They all agreed coincidence is a funny thing. While the world puts a brave face on reality, there is usually some big secret behind the façade that no one knows a damn thing about.

Soon after he married her, he painted his wife Elizabeth. Soon after that, she died. There was a little daughter, Lizzie. Soon after he painted Lizzie, she died.

'It's one of those things,' the picture tells him several times a day. Once he recovered from his grief, if he ever did, there was just one thing to do—paint himself and see what happened.

'Listen,' Foggy says. There is a noise on the stairs outside. The picture always hears it first. 'It's them,' it says. 'You might as well let them in.'

'And they the dregs of the neighbourhood?'

'They won't harm you today. They're not in that mood. No four-letter words. They just want to piss next door.' Usually Foggy is more pessimistic than this. 'It's a gang thing,' he will say. 'The ante has been upped since we were young. Nothing less than a killing will do since drugs and all that. They have dope now that would fry the best brains, not to mention a soggy mind like yours.'

The toilet is flushed. The murmur of voices rises and falls. The footsteps recede. Whoever they are, they leave an empty space and silence. Fogarty looks at the painting in consternation. That's how lonely he is, that's how desperate.

'They'll be back,' the picture promises. 'Go ahead, eat your banana.' The fruit is both breakfast and lunch because the welfare state scarcely exists and no one wants a painting since word got out that the artist is a killer. 'And now perhaps we can deal with the black eye?'

When Foggy first started talking, Fogarty held out for a year until the picture tricked him into talking back.

'What would Picasso do?' the work, at the time little more than a sketch, asked.

'I'm not Picasso,' Fogarty was lured into saying, and the conversation has not stopped since.

Now it is late afternoon, the dreamy time. Fogarty dozes until the picture alerts him that there are more footsteps on the stairs.

A discreet knock on the door is followed by a heavy pounding.

There is a young woman, nearly twenty now, named Lou. She kicked his head that night when they had him pinned down, arms outstretched, on the linoleum. There is a runt with a snotty nose. Fogarty worries about the runt, there's nothing he wouldn't do to impress his peers, if he ever had peers. Finally there is Sean, maybe nineteen, and towering, known to himself as the rebel. He was the ringleader that bad night. He is smart, for a lout, and says his philosophy is terror. He occasionally calls on Fogarty, and sometimes says he is sorry about that other time. He claims to read books, but for a rebel he is very raw and pimply and no James Dean.

'We're here to kill you, Fogarty,' the runt announces. The other two sit on a sofa, the runt on a wooden box. They have ice cream cones, two scoops each.

'Make yourselves at home,' Fogarty says, still sitting on the bed.

'Sarcastic, eh?' Lou licks her cone, then jams the beautiful ice cream into the face in the picture.

'Look at that,' the picture says to Fogarty. 'Not only third-world poverty, not only global warming, we're back to barbarism.'

Fogarty has noticed recently that the art talks a more sophisticated idiom than the artist, and this puzzles him.

'Why don't you come back and kill me another day?' he suggests wearily.

'He has a gun,' Foggy warns the dregs.

'Shut your mouth,' Fogarty hisses through broken teeth.

'Of all the pitiful predicaments, the most pitiful is to be painted by you.' The ice cream is dripping down the painting into Foggy's blue jeans.

'Have I ever told you, old man,' Sean takes over, 'about these three guys who are taken to a forest—did I ever tell you?'

'Can't say you did, Sean.'

'This really happened, Fogarty, so pay attention.' Sean prowls and rummages in the library, then the museum, until he sits down. 'This is in Germany. During the war—you probably remember it. They are two Jews and a Pole. The Germans order them to dig a hole in the forest. Then they order the two Jews into the hole. They order the Pole to fill in the hole to bury them alive.' Sean is still licking his ice cream, which occasionally drips on the worn-out amber sofa. The other two listen with interest.

'The Pole is a man with—I don't know—a conscience, I suppose. He refuses to fill the hole. So the German officer pulls out his Luger, orders the Pole into the hole.' Sean is amused by the sound of this. 'The two Jews don't waste any time filling up the hole until the clay is up to the Pole's chin. The Pole, in case you missed it, is not looking forward to what comes next. After his chin, like.'

'Go on,' the girl urges, lighting a bruised cigarette. Sadism is better than sex, she would tell you, if she had a better way with words. 'Sean is very educated,' she says to Fogarty.

'So the Germans have made their point—whatever their point was. They order the two Jews to dig out the Polack. Then they order the Jews back into the hole. The Pole has learned his lesson and does the job. The officer stomps on the grave to make sure the Jews aren't going anywhere. He looks at the Pole and the Pole looks at the ground, he's no longer a hero. So the German pulls out the Luger again and shoots him in the belly. It takes him three hours to bleed to death.'

'There you are now,' Fogarty says pointlessly.

'And would yourself like to be buried alive,' the runt asks Fogarty, 'or would you prefer the other way?'

'Don't get smart, you little punk,' the picture says. 'This man has a gun.' Fogarty glares at the picture. 'Look under the mattress if you don't believe me.' Fogarty sits on the little rusty gun for which he never had the spare money to buy ammunition.

Sean looks at Fogarty for a long time, mighty runners on his mighty feet, gaudy gear loose and greasy and the crotch down near his knees. He is fascinated by death, he will tell you after a few beers. Fogarty, though, is confident no one will hurt him today because he could never end his career with a black eye like Foggy and the ice cream dripping down.

'It's only a poem,' Sean says. 'That thing about the Pole—it's only a poem. You can look it up if you like.'

'Sean is very sophisticated,' Lou is obviously proud. 'He's not always a bad boy, are you, Sean?'

The visitors clatter down the stairs.

'Wipe me off, please,' the picture pleads.

Fogarty wipes away the ice cream. He looks around for paint, squeezes a little blue and a little zinc white from near-empty tubes. He searches for brushes, finds a couple under the bed. He mixes until he has a pale blue. He paints out the swirls and the crows over the cornfield. The background becomes blank, a world again waiting to happen. He touches up the black eye but leaves a squint, because this is still a work in progress. He tries a quick red sunrise. After years of trial and error the paint is an inch thick in places, more than that where the face is trying to break free.

'It's the drug lords,' Foggy says out of the blue. Fogarty applies a black smudge over the mouth to shut him up. 'Drug-related crimes are noted for being grisly. And while we're at it, this sunrise stinks. It might help if you put a row of trees, and me there in the shade, but then you'd have to tone down my yellow forehead.'

Sean arrives after dark accompanied by Lou, whom he calls his Muse. They are sullen and brooding. Lou smokes incessantly. Sean beats the wooden floor with a hazel stick he stole from a hardware place. 'Hey, old man.'

'Hey yourself,' Fogarty stands by the easel painting a river in the distance.

'Is it true you have a gun then?'

'Nothing to be worried about.' Fogarty produces the disabled firearm from under the mattress. 'All some guns need is ammunition but this one needs a radical overhaul.'

'We'll see about that.' Sean puts the gun in his ample pocket, while the girl tries in vain to light the peeling wallpaper with matches. Silence descends except for Sean tapping the floor with his mighty sneakers. 'Sit down,' he says.

Fogarty sits. If I live long enough I'll phone the law, he silently decides. After I get a phone. And that river is not the answer, though maybe a boat would help.

'When you die,' Sean stops tapping, 'then what happens?'

'I don't know at all.'

'Don't know?' He belts Fogarty across the side of the head with his hazel stick. 'Don't know!' And he belts him again.

Fogarty cringes, puts up his hands to protect his head. Yet he remains silent. There is nothing to be said that would do any good. A lifetime of getting hit, of falling down, of abuse and disappointment has taught him the uselessness of words, of protest, the awful scarcity of pity. When the stick does not strike a third time, he risks glancing at Sean. The stick is still poised. That's another thing about life. A poised stick can mean practically anything. A harmless stick can come alive in a jiffy. Then he has an afterthought: I'm not as hurt as I might be. Even faint hope is hope.

'When you die,' Sean says, and the stick relaxes in his hand, 'when you die, will you come back and tell us what happens?'

'Sure,' Fogarty says, without conviction.

'Does your head hurt?'

'No one has ever come back,' Fogarty ventures.

'How will I know you?' Sean pushes the misgivings aside.

'I'll meet you here. Who else could it be?'

'You'll need to look like yourself. Not like that fuckin picture.'

'Why wouldn't I?' Fogarty throws a warning glance at Foggy to be quiet.

'How soon?' This is proving easier than Sean could have imagined.

'You'd need to give me a day or two—to find out, you know, what's the score over there.'

'And you'll look like yourself, right?'

'Oh, I will. Who else would I look like?'

Sean pulls out the rusty gun. 'If you come back with a bullet in your head I'll know it's you for sure. Did you ever read Crime and Punishment?'

'Not yet.'

'A great fuckin book.'

'Sean reads everything,' Lou is peeling an orange. 'That's why he's so smart.'

'Lou is my only love,' Sean is pleased. 'It's all about love, isn't it, old dude?'

'What else could it be?' Fogarty agrees.

'We'll be back, old dude.' They quietly descend the broken stairs.

'It's all in your head,' Foggy says, 'in your crazy imagination. You never once saw them doing drugs, did you?'

'Never did.'

'Nor in possession?'

'Never.'

'You've been through a lot, you poor bastard. Elizabeth flying away.'

'That's enough.'

'Then Lizzie flying off on one wing.'

Mornings still arrive in spite of Fogarty. The sun shines again on the twelve-year-old orchard in the calendar. He picks up the dusty duds from the floor, eats a banana. He stiffens every time there is a noise on the stairs. Yet he is unable to worry about death because he can't imagine it until it happens.

He gives the dried-up river short shrift. Foggy suggests a country village with people in it, kind souls who would invite Fogarty to supper. Foggy grows more cheerful, less irritable. The dregs have not visited for several days. 'Risk it,' Foggy says. 'Try a few finishing touches.'

'Easy for you.' But he brightens the face a bit. The black eye is history. He paints blue eyes like Paul Newman's. He adds wavy hair like Clark Gable in Gone with the Wind. He removes half an inch from the ugly ear.

'A little dab of red on the lower lip,' Foggy suggests. And Fogarty indulges him, not needing to win any more battles. If a dab of red will uplift life, he won't stand in the way. He still has a fat tube of white. With it he paints over all the other backgrounds that have been years in the making: landscapes and seascapes, cornfields and clouds, places he was coming from and going to. Now it is luminous white. Foggy stands tall against this huge background, a place of unlimited possibilities.

'It's still the work of an amateur,' the picture taunts.

'It is. It's an atrocious old work of art,' Fogarty agrees. 'But in some odd way it's myself. Let them come and get me now.'

Another morning brings the cat to the window and behind the cat a yellow sun. Fogarty makes coffee. The picture says not a word but seems serene. The downstairs landlord prepares, amid din and clatter, to sell ice cream.

The lazy afternoon is interrupted by steps on the stairs. The door is thrown open. Lou comes first, followed by the runt. They seem in good spirits for dregs.

'We're here to kill you, old man,' the girl's cigarette bobs up and down between her thin lips.

'So where's Sean?'

'Dead,' she says. 'He killed himself.'

'The rusty gun worked,' the runt explains.

They sit for a while, no one saying anything, then they leave.

Fogarty and Foggy think their own thoughts.

'Go ahead,' Foggy says.

So Fogarty takes the brush again. He paints Sean into the background, going on ahead, faint in the distance, but you'd recognise the big sneakers and the hint of blood in the great white silence. Fogarty signs the picture Foggy as he used to do when he was a promising artist.

By The Book

'Next!' She spat out the word near the end of a long day.

Tap, tap, came the white cane, telltale tool of the blind. The man shuffled forward and slapped six books on the counter while the weary cane slid to the floor. Winnie looked from books to borrower: big and lumpy, nose flat like a boxer's (though she had never, to her knowledge, seen a boxer), bald on top but a fringe at the back grown straggly and bound into a flaxen pony tail. *Not our sort*, she decided. *About sixty, I'd say.*

'You need to be a member.' She looked him in the eye and thought he didn't look the least bit blind.

'To be or not to be,' solemnly he imitated Hamlet.

'If you wish to borrow books, that is.' Despite all the stereotypes going around, there is no stereotypical librarian. But if there were, Winnie would be a candidate: spinster with porcelain face and thin red lips that did not need lipstick; suspiciously black hair (for forty-eight). Demure on the outside. On the inside: turmoil. In theory she was in favour of reading, including the books in her own library. But, in practice, she resented readers.

'How much?' He asked in a hoarse, damaged voice. Every book borrower was unsuitable in a different way. Winnie disliked this fellow's assumption that money was an issue. *Which, however, it is.*

'Name?'

'White. Wilbur White.' She wrote it on a yellow form. He gave a local address.

'Are you new to the area, then?'

'No.' A more agreeable sort would have explained why, at this juncture, he suddenly needed no less than six books. But she let that pass, proud of her patience, she could always outfox these people in the end.

'Occupation?'

'I follow the blind dog.'

'I beg your pardon?'

'Over the twisted trail.' It was the last straw, though she feared other last straws would follow.

He signed the form she pushed in front of him. *Voila, he can see that much. Though the signature did stray. Though that, too, could be a ruse.* He spoke in sign language to a woman behind him, small and tidy as he was big and loose, deaf or he would talk to her; and dumb, otherwise she would talk to him. *Sad*, Winnie thought in an unguarded moment. *Not my problem*, she then reminded herself.

The Crooked Timber of Humanity by Isaiah Berlin sat on top of his pile. Winnie prided herself on being acquainted with every book in the library. Yet she could not recall this one.

Tragedy and the Theory of Drama by Elder Olson was next. *Don't dare ask. Give him an inch and he'll prattle ad nauseam.* He meanwhile stared over Winnie's head where there was a print by Mondrian on the wall. *That's the great thing about abstract art; you don't need to see it.*

The next book was *Small Is Beautiful* by E. F. Schumacher. *Sure, I heard of it, but I didn't know we had it.* On the cover the earth was emerging from an eggshell. She played her laser beam over the bar code. *All this intense material. What a mind he must have. There's just one thing. He can't read.*

Dreams of a Final Theory by Steven Weinberg came next. Now he's showing off. 'The Scientist's Search for the Ultimate Laws of

Nature,' this one explained. *Ultimate my eye.*

'Isn't it a grand day now.' One was expected to be civil, and furthermore she had found such innocent remarks often broke the ice once people discovered you were not the enemy.

'Yes, indeed.' And added: 'People were never meant to live indoors. Now they're forgetting how it once was under the skies. Anyone can see where that will lead.'

'Where?' she couldn't help asking.

'Do you open on Sundays?' he pointedly changed the subject.

'Of course not,' she replied in a huffy way. For a moment they had almost made contact. They were within a few words of sharing something significant, then the day fell back into incoherence. 'Declan!' she called to her assistant, because a line had formed.

She could be surprisingly affected by the books people borrowed. When fat Ginny Adams checked out steamy romances, it was impossible to deny that love of all sorts took place behind closed doors. At the end of a day, bombarded by a constant mix of wisdom and nonsense, Winnie was usually an emotional basket case.

Next she ran the laser over *The Gift* by Lewis Hyde, yet another work that had escaped her notice. 'Imagination and the Erotic Life of Property,' the preposterous subtitle said. She would explore these books just as soon as he returned them. *Life would be simpler if people borrowed the same books. Of which there are far too many anyway.* Winnie had a degree in library science and could rattle off the great libraries from ancient Babylon to the Bodleian. She had studied enough to know that most books were either useless or redundant. She once wrote a letter to the *Library Journal* suggesting an ombudsman who would alert people to the sheer repetition in most libraries. This created such an outcry that she never again risked airing her thoughts.

Wilbur White's final book was a Tolstoy novel. *Wouldn't you know, not a bit run of the mill.* She saw by the date-due form that it had not been borrowed for eleven years. *That must surely say something. About the common sense of readers. About this new customer. And, while we're at it, about Tolstoy.* She had dusted this book year after year but had never been tempted to read it. Not that she was illiterate. She had gone back to school for a master's in English literature. She could blind you with erudition about Milan Kundera and Gabriel Garcia Marquez and (if you're still stuck back there) Shakespeare. Not that she enjoyed these, nor yet that she was edified by them—she felt her special gift to the library profession, her charism, was precisely the fact that she did not go gaga over books.

'There you go.' She slapped Tolstoy on top of the other five. *I wonder.* She excused herself. From the front office she spied on them. If he were to get behind the wheel, after that pathetic show of blindness, her professional pessimism would be vindicated. But it was the little woman who drove, her chin high. *Sorry*, Winnie said in a whisper to the universe, *sometimes life is what it seems.* For a brief moment she felt good that *War and Peace* was getting an airing.

I'd marry him in a minute. She returned to her counter. *But then there's the other woman. I don't know how to be deaf and dumb, just for starters, I wouldn't suit him.*

She copied his address and slipped it in her pocket. *Professionalism is all I have left and now that's slipping away.* She drove past Wilbur White's house in her Toyota. It was a small house, white and tidy. *And he so big.*

He was back in a week, tap, tap, she didn't need to look up.

'I hope you enjoyed the books.' It was a perfectly acceptable thing to say.

The woman became his eyes foraging through the bookstacks. Winnie could not imagine by what arcane process they chose another four books. Except that it had been years since any of the four was borrowed.

Gradually the professional crisis grew in Winnie's psyche. There was some great waste here. Most books were ignored most of the time. Trees had been cut down to make paper for these books. An elaborate printing process was set in motion to spell out line after line of book after book. Before that there was the lonely toil of writers, slow word after slow word, half the words crossed out again without seeing the light of day. Scratch of the pen, wheezy drone of the computer. Winnie had tried it; she knew what was involved. Worse was the huxtering of a finished manuscript to editors and agents. Then the interminable wait for rejection. Or occasional elation when the publishing world trembled and someone said yes. Followed by a further tiny shiver when a newspaper reviewed it. Then began the spotty life of the book. One in a million was cherished in rare homes, an idea whose time had come, while the others were lined up cheek by jowl to moulder on the shelves of libraries like her own.

'Not many borrow this one,' she ventured as she stamped *The Psychology of War* by Lawrence LeShan.

'No one at all,' he assured her.

He was back in four days. Then in three. She yearned to ask him how he did whatever he did—read or not read them. As his routine picked up speed she figured he could borrow the whole library in a couple of years. Yet he was excruciatingly selective. One day they borrowed a dozen, carrying six each. These included Colin Wilson's *The Outsider*. 'Luminously intelligent,' a quote declared on the front cover, 'truly astonishing.' *Exaggerated, to be sure*. But she was impatient to have the book back and see for herself.

Then he came daily. *There's no law against it*. Not only that: there was a growing satisfaction at seeing the books circulate. The thing most unbecoming to books was to be ignored: a repudiation of their very purpose. Winnie pondered these vague intellectual stirrings. *What if I have a mission, a vocation?* She read voraciously to get ahead of Wilbur White. It was embarrassing, in her position, to be following the lead of a blind man. She started making lists, moving books around, moving furniture around, making posters with messages: 'If You Read Only One

Book, Let It Be This One.' That book would then fly off the shelf. The community picked up the buzz. People began to greet Winnie on the street. *It's destiny.*

On a Monday morning she packed several hundred selected books in cardboard boxes and ordered dumbfounded Declan to put them in her car.

'Look after the store,' she admonished as she drove away. On the passenger seat she had spread a map of the area.

'I'm your local librarian,' she said at the first door. 'I happen to know you don't use the library.' The problem was what to say. 'Why don't I leave you half a dozen for starters?'

'Is this a practical joke?' Questions passed like clouds across the woman's face.

'Have you ever read the novels of John McGahern?'

'Not yet. I have eight grandchildren.'

If she invites me in, I'll drink the cup of coffee, whatever it takes. 'I also have history and technology and memoirs. And if you wish to be more daring I'd recommend a biography of Friedrich Nietzsche, the philosopher. Quite odd, actually, but a genius. "One must have chaos within oneself to give birth to a dancing star." He wrote that.'

'But what does it mean?'

'Oh, I wouldn't go looking for anything as ordinary as meaning in the case of Mr Nietzsche. It's more a matter of, I don't know, of insight, I suppose.'

'I'll give it a whirl,' the woman said. *I've died and gone to heaven.* Winnie recorded the woman's particulars on her laptop. She noted that the book had been borrowed twice from the library five years ago. After that, nothing. This was no way to run the world. Nietzsche had gone crazy before he died, and no wonder, he probably suspected the centuries of neglect that lay ahead.

The next three houses came up empty. Outside the third a car was parked, which made her suspicious. 'I know you're in there,' she said in a girlish voice through the brass letter box. *I would never have done that in a million years. Something has come over me and, bless my soul, I'm enjoying it.*

'I think, perhaps, Albert Camus,' she said to a young couple. 'I have *Exile and the Kingdom*, and several copies of *The Stranger*, a classic. But that's just an opinion. You might prefer religion, or historical romances.' She hoped to shame them into going for quality. 'It's not as if you have to read them.' So they took ten. By noon she had lent three hundred books. She would return in three weeks, she told people. They smiled various smiles, from sincere to sarcastic. *Yet there's something bigger going on here.* Some of the best authors who ever lived were, she knew, beholden to her that day.

By the end of a week many of the library shelves were bare. An urgency grew on people.

'When will you be doing our street?'

'I'll be down on Saturday. Would poetry interest you?'

'I haven't looked at poetry since school.'

'I'd suggest an American called Mona Van Duyn. Listen to this:

> What is love? Truly I do not know.
> Sometimes, perhaps, instead of a great sea,
> it is a narrow stream running urgently.

See what I mean?'

'I'll have that one, to be sure,' the other party said. And Winnie threw in a history of China because, she said, 'for centuries the Chinese never existed, not that you'd notice.'

'You're pulling my leg,' the other party grinned, happy to be conned.

I'll run for office. There is a whole population out here waiting to be led.

There were glitches. Books went missing. Winnie hired an assistant for the over-worked Declan. Autumn darkened into winter, the time for reading. No one could recall such book mania ever happening before. *Books always go missing. What matters is that they are lost in a good cause, like dead soldiers. And as for turmoil, it must mean we're still alive.* Winnie traded in her car for a van. *What should not be overlooked is that I'm happier than ever before.*

Several weeks into her odyssey, she came to the house of Wilbur White. The little woman invited her in. Wilbur sat looking into a fire.

'It didn't seem proper to pass without saying hello.'

'Ah, yes.' There were no books in sight.

'I generally recommend books, but you two know what you want.' The little woman brought a glass of sherry. 'It wasn't about the books,' Winnie said. 'It was about doing something. People were living one day after another as if it didn't matter, while every morning, if the truth be told, was the beginning of a new century.' *I'm talking rubbish, but why wouldn't I, I'm nervous.*

'Fire down below,' Wilbur White fingered the white cane fiercely.

'I'm sorry?'

'The wind in the willows, the heart of the matter, the cat and canary, I'd read them if I could see them.' His big face was innocent as an old angel's.

'I'm truly glad to have met you.' Winnie stood to go.

'I'm glad to have met you, too,' he said with perfect poise.

They shook hands. *I'll persist until someone thinks of firing me. After so long a time, no one knows what to do with books once they've been written. And when they do fire me I'll write a fab reference for Declan, who has not had an idea for years. He'll be ideal.*

Catharina

A saw flashed in the morning light and the urgent sound rose and fell like the scratchy call of a corncrake. When the branch could stand it no longer it crashed with a shudder into Igoe's field. She adjusted the ladder and attacked another limb. She was mightier than any man in the county, the men said. But very much a woman, they would add—although I was only thirteen, I knew what they meant. She wore a black cap with a glossy sunshade, and sure enough the sun edged inquisitively over the horizon. The air was clear as in the early days of creation. Her breath created a whiff of vapour in the cold morning. She must be hot inside, I thought, like a volcano, to create steam like that. Odd what one remembers.

She sawed off several more branches until the bare arm of the sycamore seemed to flex lumpy muscles over the field. The countryside squinted to see what would happen next. She climbed the ladder with an old kettle dangling on a rope. Then she carried a washboard aloft, a wizened face painted on the corrugated surface, and it bobbed foolishly from the gnarly bough. Beside the washboard she hung a dead black cat, spinning slowly, the front paws clawing the air to get back to earth. In the end there were six objects, adorned with colours one seldom sees in trees. That old townland had survived sleepy and unnoticed for thousands of years until she set foot in it.

Across the field, hunkered down behind a swarthy oak, Felix

Foran watched her, still as a rock, wily as a druid, a drab druid with a drip from his nose. His breath, compared with Catharina's, was a patch of stale old steam.

I was watching the two of them from behind a tree of my own.

'I saw you, Tiger,' she taunted that evening, her large lips laughing.

'But you didn't see Felix,' I crowed, giving the druid's game away. I was old-fashioned for my age.

The village was agog when word spread that an artist had rented the Hanly farmhouse. A woman at that. Annie Hanly fed rumours to the locals like oats to hungry hens. British, Annie said. Or maybe Russian, with a name like Catharina. She didn't tell us that Catharina would arrive on a monster motorcycle, a blood red Royal Enfield, with a sidecar hopping along beside it from pothole to pothole.

She was dressed in black leather gear and high boots up near her knees. This ensemble was crowned by a futuristic helmet with shiny plastic visor. In a flamboyant gesture, she pulled off the helmet and a huge crop of golden hair cascaded over her shoulders and kept on going.

'I'm looking for the Hanly place,' she announced at our door.

The road forks in the middle of our village. My mother owned the lounge bar, called The Old Goat, situated in the fork in the road. Out front were petrol pumps. Behind the bar was a general store, everything in it from shovels to Easter eggs. Down a corridor was what we called the snug, a sombre little room with a faded picture of the pope on one wall, where shy parishioners could enjoy a whiskey before heading home on the bicycle.

'You must be the artist.' My mother, a romantic, gave every newcomer a shot of whiskey on the house. Make a wish, she would say. Catharina looked at that whiskey until I thought she had fallen into a trance. Then she downed it with the fierce suddenness of a gunslinger—I was reading Zane Gray at the time and seeing the world through the eyes of Buck Duane. It was obvious this blow-in had made a mighty wish and we'd better watch out.

Several locals were already nursing pints of porter, trying to make peace with the day. I could soon see that any one of them would give his life for Catharina if only he could find an excuse. The artist rewarded this chivalry with a wave in their direction and a shake of her head that sent the hair cascading again. Any room she entered became a warmer but also a more mysterious place. She had surprisingly large lips, curved and perfect, and shiny teeth like Belleek porcelain.

'She's a swashbuckling woman,' Healy said around three o'clock, after Catharina had eased herself out the road on the sputtering motorcycle. Once the coast was clear, the village stalwarts converged on The Old Goat thirsty for gossip. Healy's garage was directly across the road, but he never made it to work that day. By nightfall everyone had an opinion of the new artist, imagination taking over from memory and hearsay until she was larger than life.

'There never was a painter painted these parts before.'

'She can paint me any time she wants.'

'She'd never be that hard up. They usually paint clamps of turf or old outhouses. Especially if there's a touch of colour, like a red front door. Or something out of the ordinary, like turkeys, I tell you no lie, artists love swans on a lake, or horses galloping, they're devils for horses galloping.'

My mother pulled pints for them. When the talk got arty, Master Keene and Healy turned to drinking wine. By closing time they were planning an exhibition of her paintings in the parish hall. In a far corner I pretended to do my homework, but privately I had decided homework was no longer necessary because I was going to be an artist.

'Go out and see is she all right,' my mother said, when Catharina failed to appear for three days. I found her on top of the Hanly house painting big white blobs on the roof.

'Annie Hanly won't like this.'

'They're planets,' she said, and the beautiful teeth shone. 'That one there is Jupiter. And here's the moon.'

'The moon isn't a planet. It's just a moon.' On the cobbled driveway the motorcycle waited; it seemed a waste not to be riding somewhere. She asked would I like a glass of lemonade. I declined, eager to get back to The Old Goat and tell everyone about the planets on her roof. My friend Charlie Gibbons said this was a mistake because after the lemonade, anything could happen. There was a lascivious glint in his under-age eye.

'I'll have that lemonade now if you don't mind,' I said the next day. She was arranging thin laths painted in bright colours, the whole rainbow.

'You'll have to earn it first.' So off we went with the laths into Igoe's field. She stuck them in the ground at certain points, counting her steps, then tramped into the next field and hammered home more of the same. I thought all this was a little daft, but then I figured, if I was going to be an artist, it was easier than painting horses galloping.

'What are you doing?'

'Sending messages.' A couple of pigeons flapped from a low tree. Pigeons weren't blind, they couldn't miss what was going on. Catharina wore a denim dress down to her toes with the nails painted green.

'She's sending messages,' I announced in the lounge that evening. The next day, coloured sticks were sighted at Lissogue crossroads. There followed a procession of neighbours wanting to see for themselves. Felix Foran came down from the mountain, which in reality is only a hill, and said the 'monstrosities' were planted all the way to the summit.

'You'd be better off painting pictures.' I had cycled out on the Saturday.

'What do you mean, pictures?'

'Like horses galloping. Or old outhouses.'

The sun still had miles to go the following Thursday when the roar of her motorcycle brought the village to life. Queen Maeve was said to have come from our part of the West, and Healy said Catharina on the motorcycle reminded him of Maeve on a dun steed. She removed the helmet with a deft twist as if she were taking off her head, and lobbed it into the sidecar.

'Hey Tiger,' she said, making me the envy of the village.

The neighbourhood got unaccountably thirsty and converged on The Old Goat. Catharina, enthroned on a tall stool, gave an occasional shake of the lovely hair and smiled the huge smile and said hello to anyone bold enough to look her in the eye. She wore a black sweater with the collar up around her long neck, and from her ears dangled long copper earrings, the kind Queen Maeve would have worn.

It was awkward for a while. The usual bigmouths had nothing to say. Remarks were made about the weather. Catharina said the village was 'quaint,' but no one risked asking what she meant.

'You have us all guessing about them coloured sticks,' Healy then said, and the conversation took off like a runaway horse.

The 1970s were waving goodbye to the 1960s. Those who wanted Catharina to paint traditional landscapes had no idea how art had gone crazy for nearly a century. There was Impressionism and Cubism, Fauvism and Surrealism, and more. Artists were supposed to break new ground, otherwise art would die. Instead of a woman's face, artists needed to get under her skin, maybe take a look at her soul. It took a different kind of artist to think up Futurism and the like, not to mention abstract art that seemed to be about nothing but might be about everything. That kind of thing took a Kandinsky or a Picasso, giants.

I myself knew little of these matters. Master Keene and others nodded eagerly while Catharina did most of the talking. Healy would ask stupid questions to keep the talk going. She would look from one face to the next, leaving no one out, the ivory teeth flashing and the huge eyes roving back and forth and her long-fingered hands making extravagant moves.

One thing led to another, she said. When artists got tired painting what was outside their heads they painted what was inside, and found some odd surprises there. Some threw away their brushes. They found any old stuff and stuck it together and put it in galleries, where it sold.

'And don't forget conceptual art.' She went on about minimalism and body art. Every so often, someone would wink at my mother, who would quietly nudge another glass of beer in front of her.

'It's all bloody nonsense,' Felix Foran said when she stopped to sip the beer.

'Get this man another drink,' Catharina said, disarming him, and my mother set a large whiskey in front of Felix.

It got boisterous after that. I was sent to bed. Catharina got drunk and danced with several farmers. Modern art arrived late in the deep West but it arrived the way art should, with controversy knocking heads together. We were a generation behind more advanced parts of the world. It was hard to see how hanging a washboard and a dead cat from a tree could shake up a community. This is because of the layers of local history buried deep under people's skin, Catharina told me. Like the layers of an onion, she said. I had become practically her right hand man by the end of a month. For thousands of years the local psyche had sailed along undisturbed, she said. Then one day coloured sticks were sprouting in the fields and people who grew up on omens were worried.

Igoe came storming to her house on his bike and demanded she take down the dead cat. She hung a bottle of perfume in place of the stinking animal. Two nights later, the perfume disappeared.

'Art is alive,' she explained. 'It's not always predictable.'

When April came she bought an old car without doors. With Healy's help, she engineered it to go in circles around Igoe's field, all by itself, until it ran out of petrol. She filled it up and off the car went again.

First the villagers came out and sat on the stone wall to watch. Then the local farmers arrived, smoking pipes and muttering. By Saturday, there was a picture in the paper and people coming from three counties away to see the sensational machine which created an eerie glow at night which everyone pretended had a perfectly natural explanation.

Catharina did not seem to notice. She had already moved on to making a wigwam in front of the farmhouse. The talk grew more intense: what would happen next?

'Art is about what will happen next, Tiger,' she seemed to read my mind. 'It's not about reinventing the wheel.'

Igoe became alarmed and ordered the car removed from his field. The dumb vehicle sat sulking on empty. Then word spread she had bought Igoe's field. She stuck a For Sale sign on the car and an art dealer from Holland bought it.

Occasionally she would still visit The Old Goat. Soon the place would be full. Very few women ever frequented the pub, so she had the lads to herself.

'What are you up to now, Catharina?'

She would get them singing old country songs. When they insisted, she would sing a song or two of her own in some foreign tongue. She said it was French but we knew enough to know it wasn't. She could fill the lounge with sound, like mighty divas in the operas my mother watched on television.

'I need you first thing in the morning, Tiger.' She never called anybody else Tiger. Like all the men of the parish, I would have died for her. The following day, with two fat brushes, we painted the Igoe field blue.

'A sprayer would be better.' The brush was slow and monotonous.

'But it wouldn't be art.'

'Is it some message we're sending?'

'It sort of is.'

'And who's the message for?'

'Did I ever tell you about the French artist Matisse?' There were some questions she wouldn't answer. 'They called him a wild beast because they couldn't tame him.'

'How, tame him?'

'Matisse would have painted this field pink.' She had a big spacious mind and strange ideas rattled around in it from morning to night. It was impossible to predict which ideas would slip out into the real world. 'But it would be wrong to imitate Matisse.' Then she told me about a Russian architect who designed the fabulous Saint Basil's Cathedral in Red Square. The czar feared he might design another cathedral for someone else, maybe a grander one, so he put out the architect's eyes.

The Igoe field took all day to paint. The hubbub started early, cars stopping and drivers gawking, before rushing off to tell others. As for myself, I have never since spent such an exuberant springtime. What did she say, the men would ask at night in The Old Goat. Why was she doing it? And I would tell them a little at a time, tickling their curiosity: about the wild artist Matisse and the unfortunate Russian who designed too grand a cathedral for his own good.

'There's something fishy about that woman.' In the old days Felix Foran seldom darkened the pub door, but lately he was sucking a pint every night.

'She's only an artist, Felix.' My mother wanted the public house to be a haven for the poor devils, as she called them—she herself had not fared well in the domestic bliss department. She tried to keep The Old Goat magical, all glass and mirrors, bottles glinting, rows upon rows of promise. Nearly everyone drank ordinary porter, but the exotic bottles were a guarantee—like heaven, in a way—that a higher order existed when people were willing and able.

'That's no excuse,' Felix said. No one ever gave backchat to my mother. Yet something was simmering under the surface of our lives.

President Kennedy had promised to send a man to the moon. Although Kennedy was dead the mighty aspiration lived on. Space vehicles were launched as the USA tried to keep up with the Communists. John Glen went aloft and said outer space was safe as far as the eye could see. Speculation grew about what might be out beyond the sky. Healy had painted a monster bull's-eye on the roof of his garage, in case aliens should be passing. He claimed business had doubled.

The village seemed to be holding its breath in anticipation of something unspecified. New ideas trickled down mysterious boreens to impoverished fields. Journalists came in shiny cars to see Catharina's creations. When glossy magazines appeared with new features, neighbours would shake their heads in pride as if they had a hand in it. Which they had, Catharina insisted. Master Keene let his hair grow to his shoulders, while Healy took to wearing a black beret.

Early one Saturday morning, I could hear the farting of the motorcycle coming closer. I was out of bed in a bound, pulling on the dirty jeans as I staggered down the stairs. Catharina rapped imperiously on the stained-glass door. She was wearing her leather gear and high boots.

'Up and at it, Tiger.'

'Up and at what?' I always gave her a certain amount of lip, refusing to follow the trend of swooning over her.

'In there.' It was my first time in the sidecar. She handed me ancient goggles, black and exotic such as pilots wore in the big war. We headed for the mountain. Half way up, she left the rough, narrow road for a rougher one, then did a further zig and zag before circling to a stop behind a clump of whins. The silence was intense. Catharina detached a knapsack from the pillion, threw it over her shoulder. She was more nimble on the mountain than Felix Foran's goats. I followed her between the rocks and sheep droppings, too out of my element even to ask questions.

Near the top, in a rocky alcove, she unloaded a green outfit from the knapsack.

'Put it on,' she ordered. The outfit had eyes on stilts on top of my head. It's all a blur now, but I remember a battery strapped to my back, and lights flashing. She led me to a rock on the summit. 'You're scaring the hell out of me,' she said, 'you look like someone from Neptune or Mars.'

Art was a mystery. Galloping horses were for amateurs like Master Keene. I looked down at our own toy village sleepy in the sunlight. Catharina and I were making mysterious art, but it wouldn't be worth a damn if neighbours failed to notice an extraterrestrial in their midst.

'I have to pee,' I blurted out, embarrassed—Michelangelo or Matisse would never need to go at a time like this.

'Of course you do,' she said, as if peeing were part of the process. I did what I had to do against a whin bush while raddled sheep stared at our human folly. When I turned around the mischievous Catharina was nowhere to be seen.

It's a blur now, as I say, blurred by time and pain and incomprehension. I stood like a statue on the plinth on which she had set me. It was thrilling for a while, waiting to be discovered like every artist's work. Then, getting tired, I shifted my weight from one leg to the other. Eventually I did a full turn, so that villagers, if they ever looked, would be looking for the first time in their lives at an alien backside.

Then there he was, the inevitable Felix Foran, crawling on hands and knees between the rocks. The devil got into me and I raised my arm the way his followers used to salute Hitler, just for a moment, then returned to being a statue. Felix turned tail down the mountain. This was further evidence that art was powerful and could make things happen.

Soon the locals arrived en masse. They scampered furtively from ancient rock to whitethorn hedge. I stood still as long as I could, then saluted as before. This manoeuvre kept them at bay. I longed for Catharina to reappear but she was as invisible as God. Fear began to gnaw. If I proved to be less than extraterrestrial, they would beat the tar out of me by sundown. Whether in memory or imagination, the standoff lasted until the village in dribs and drabs went home to the tea.

At last Catharina came from the shadows and hugged me and said I was a star. There was a full moon. The first astronauts had just landed there, a couple of Americans leaping about in their swollen spacesuits. I wished they would look down and see me, they could do it if they wanted, with their amazing binoculars and know-how. But that was a thing about art: you could only do so much, then everything depended on what others saw.

The village was edgy and uncertain. In the bar there was not the usual excitement and jackassing. Still, when Catharina came waltzing in, a grinning big tomboy, she was irresistible. Soon she had a sing-song going. An old farmer sang quietly in the *sean-nós* idiom, haunting the place. Catharina sang in her own foreign tongue, and I could see the men still loved her.

Then a bullock died in O'Rian's field. It was not uncommon for a beast to die, but the nervous mood led to muttering. Word circulated of other incidents, each with its own quite logical explanation.

'Don't be daft,' Healy said. 'Little green men wouldn't harm an animal.'

'Who said anything about little green men?'

My mother, after resisting for years, allowed TV in the lounge. Soon everyone in the parish had a set. One could see the difference in local thinking. Old-timers stopped talking about mythical events when the world was young, like cows calving or blind bards singing. The conversation turned to English soccer or the war in Vietnam.

Felix Foran's life had been no more conspicuous than the undersize mountain he lived on. Had he died at any other time his death wouldn't have caused a ripple. But speculation was in the air, everyone circumspect. The guards called in a doctor in case of foul play. The funeral was small. Among the few following the coffin was Catharina, dressed in black and a stiff hat atop the beautiful hair. She walked with head erect in silent solemnity. I got bold and walked beside her, but there was no bantering with Tiger on this unexpected occasion.

'And didn't he go fast?' In the lounge, in the days that followed, Felix was remembered in a guarded way.

'The heart, I'd say.' The conversation would always stop short of playing itself out. Then it would start up again, as if something more needed to be said.

'And did you see Catharina?'

'Wasn't that an odd thing, too?'

Catharina did not appear for several days. I longed for her to arrive in a cloud of dust and sit on some farmer's lap and tell everyone not to worry because modern art was going through a phase while it waited for a more heroic world to celebrate.

'Go out and take a look,' my mother said after a week.

The blue door was ajar. A black-and-white cat sat sleepy on the wide saddle of the motorcycle. I had not known about this snooty companion. I then realised there must be a whole other world to which Catharina belonged, about which I knew nothing, including family and friends and faraway places, one of which must surely be her home.

She usually came to the door to welcome me with her happy face and the Tiger lingo. Round at the back was an old barn where she concocted her art. I pressed my nose against the big window. The place was cluttered with bric-a-brac. No one could guess what new wonders it would become some sunny day.

'Hello!' I said from the yard. Only silence came back. I went through the door with a louder hello. The kitchen was tidy. 'Catharina!' I now shouted. It was the first time I had called her by her name. There was a door to the parlour at one end and to the bedroom at the other. I knocked on each in turn, knocked in vain. I made no effort to open them. Puzzlement grew into fear. I cycled home through a tangle of emotions. I would look foolish if I raised a false alarm. Things were seldom what they seemed,

Catharina loved to say. Yet what if she were behind one of those doors? The premonition grew.

Everyone at The Old Goat dismissed my misgivings. Then everyone started a vigil just in case. For a night and a day the locals cycled out for a look, or did a detour on the way home. A few took up positions in the bushes. These manoeuvres were never discussed. Suspicion spread like a fog across the parish. Catharina might be up to her tricks again, that was one option. Meanwhile, the blue door remained open. The motorcycle sat brooding, and so did the cat.

The guards were notified. They searched the house. No, they said, there was nothing further to report. She was, after all, a celebrity, and the last thing we needed was a spotlight on the village. On the other hand, reality had to be faced. A young guard took my mother and me into the snug for questioning. This served to remind me how little I knew. I wanted to tell them the Royal Enfield was rusting and should be in from the weather, but I worried lest some legal loose end might land me in jail.

After a week the guards organised a search party. The media descended. There was never one day when she was officially gone or dead or disappeared. We had no suitable word for her situation. After a further week the media, and with the media the wide world, lost interest. There was no dead body. Though no live one, either. And no body of work. Catharina's art was as ephemeral as ideas that run wild in the world.

For months the guards cruised slowly on the narrow roads. They did not seem to be going anywhere, just waiting and observing.

The more Catharina was forgotten by the outside world, the more her legend grew in the deep West. At first the people were confused or sad or angry. No one ever mentioned that she was dead, just that she was gone. There was, accordingly, immense scope for recreating her as weeks passed into months and years.

'Do you mind that time she stuck spuds like apples on

Hanly's apple tree?' Not everyone remembered everything, and as time passed it seemed disrespectful to have forgotten so soon.

'Oh, begod, I remember well. And the McWeeneys coming in the dead of night and picking the spuds for apple tarts.'

One Saturday, when new grass was getting the upper hand, a few men went out and painted the field blue again. I imagined how happy that would make her, and hoped her message was at last reaching its destination.

'I keep wishing,' a farmer voiced our common thought, 'for her to come through that door and get everyone laughing again, and singing, and all the old codology.'

'Tell me, Martin, did she ever sit on your lap?'

'I have to admit, she never did.'

'Faith now, she sat on mine.'

Sometimes the talk would turn grim.

'She didn't just go straight up to heaven.' No one mentioned murder. They talked around the periphery. Felix Foran's name would often come up.

'Sure, wasn't Felix dead ahead of her.'

'Don't I know.'

'That old bike,' someone would then steer the talk back to higher ground. 'Do you remember how she used to pull off that helmet, and all the hair would fall down?' Eyes would grow shiny with the memory.

'That art is dangerous,' a gaunt farmer said one night from under his hat. 'She should have stuck to painting thatched cottages.'

'There are no thatched cottages left to paint, Barney.'

'Mountains, then. There's mountains left.'

As the legend seeped into the communal memory, the conclusion grew inevitable that her art had brought some unspecified tragedy on Catharina. Healy had been reading up on artists and found a surprising number of them came to an untidy end.

'Could it be extraterrestrial forces?' Master Keene suggested. It would be such a relief to lay the blame elsewhere.

'Closer to home, I'd say,' the gaunt farmer said. This caused a hush. Whenever it got past closing time in the village, my mother would turn out the lights and the conversation would continue in the interminable twilight.

'I heard they put her eyes out first.'

'Who?'

'Whoever it was.'

'There was no body,' I spoke up one night from the corner where I was studying algebra. They stared at me in disbelief, the late-night drinkers, old men huddled around a mystery.

Her blinded eyes echoed the tale of the Russian architect destroyed by the czar. Prehistoric crimes were mentioned and unmentionable details suggested, including more up-to-date outrages committed by sinister forces. Neighbours, in short. I was only thirteen, my imagination young and limber. A day came when I could no longer be sure. Was it memory or imagination that she was lying on the floor in her dried blood, her poor perfect mouth kissing the kitchen linoleum? On bad days I can be haunted by regret that I didn't rescue her, didn't talk to her, didn't hold the hand that twitched and pleaded, didn't even put a blanket over her before cycling back in panic to the village.

But on good days I know Catharina escaped us to start over and become a star far away, under a new *nom de guerre*, after turning our village into her finest work of art.

Gravity

Once you take seriously that all possible universes can (or do) exist, then a slippery slope opens up before you. It has long been recognized that technical civilizations, only a little more advanced than ourselves, will have the capability to simulate universes in which self-conscious entities can emerge and communicate with one another… Once this capability to simulate universes is achieved, fake universes will proliferate and will soon greatly outnumber the real ones. Thus, Nick Bostrom has argued that a thinking being here and now is more likely to be in a simulated reality than a real one.

—John D. Barrow: *The Artful Universe Expanded* (Oxford University Press, 2005)

Kyle Wihry sat on a stone outside a hotel called Gershwins drinking an orange beverage and observing the sunset on the last day of a conference on alcoholism. He was covering the conference for a newspaper called, like many others, *The Star*. He was, at the time, sixty, with the slight stoop sixty years often bring. Unruly rusty hair encroached on his forehead. He wore an ill-fitting white suit of a kind favoured by certain dandies in the writing trade. His mind wandered as the weary sun eased itself into a cushion of cloud.

Then, in the middle distance, a house rose into the air.

Events that seldom or never happen are more difficult to put into words because no one ever needed to invent a vocabulary for them. In this case it was easier to say what did not happen. The house did not explode. It did not grow instant wings. It was not hoisted into the sky by a helicopter or other technology. And yet into the sky was precisely where it was going, rising slowly like a hot-air balloon. Eventually it caught the rays of the sinking sun. It looked like a two-storey, though, for the moment, the usual certainties no longer applied. Pieces seemed to fall away, part of the foundation perhaps, or floorboards or flower pots— who knew what would hold together in a situation like this.

Kyle did a quick psychological inventory: I'm not going crazy; I'm not drunk; I didn't fall asleep. No one was rushing out of the hotel to see this wonder. Yet there the house was, wafting in the direction of a few white clouds, and eventually enveloped. He waited for it to reappear, but it did not, and the evening returned to normal. He resisted the urge to rush into the hotel and shout the news. Amazing things often had perfectly normal explanations, though rarely in the history of earth did something as abnormal as this actually happen.

He hurried to the rented car. There should be no trouble finding where the house had been. There was bound to be a hubbub.

He drove around the suburb for an hour, first at random, then systematically. But there was no hubbub, no consternation. People were out walking, others driving. They seemed neither excited nor otherwise abnormal. He was tempted to stop and ask them, but what would he say? 'Did you see the house taking off?' He couldn't do it. He could try something more roundabout. 'Are you sure there was no one trapped in that house that went sailing away?' But no one wants to be regarded as a nut case, even by strangers. They say the person going bonkers is the last to know. But damn it, he concluded, I saw it.

He drove back slowly to the hotel. The news would be on television, probably with a disappointingly simple explanation.

'So how was the conference?' Beth asked when he got home.

'Boring, it was boring.'

They had been married thirty-five years. They had exhausted all the surprises and settled on domestic formulae that saw them through the day. He knew Beth didn't want to hear about the alcohol conference—unless something startling had happened. He couldn't tell her about the floating house, not until there was confirmation, because Beth didn't suffer fools lightly. He checked his computer, checked CNN on the hour, and was rewarded with the usual litany of trivia that passed for news.

Kyle was not a gregarious man. While he did not dislike people, he seldom warmed to them, except to romance Beth until three children resulted and life became routine again. This remoteness made it easier to keep his secret to himself.

A week later, a rival paper reported that an airline pilot had seen from his cockpit a cow high in the sky. Kyle had been scooped.

'It must have been dead,' the pilot said, 'but how it got there, or why it didn't fall back to earth, well, your guess is as good as mine.'

Kyle searched the media but could find no confirmation of the cow story. The pilot might have taken an illicit drink before take-off.

'Did you see that story about the cow?' he asked Beth over the lasagna.

'What story?' She was thin and taut. She had bulging eyes, caused, Kyle was convinced, by peering too long and intensely at computers, her profession and passion. She hid behind bronze-tinted glasses that, she said, allowed her to stare down the computer without frying her brain—her terminology turned esoteric when she talked technology. When the children went into the world one at a time, Beth, born, she insisted, to be a mother, was bereft. She seemed to be waiting for the next worthwhile thing—though Kyle felt he wasn't it. Thus a distance had grown between them, a no-man's land. They bridged this gap on good days, especially when the children visited. But mostly they were cautious, waiting until both were in the mood for whatever it was, banter or business or, occasionally, intimacy.

'In the paper. A pilot saw a cow at thirty thousand feet.'

'That's not possible, dear.'

'Of course it's not possible. I'm just telling you what was in the paper.' That settled it. He could not tell her about the house that had taken off at low speed.

'Some people like to bring attention to themselves.'

'Or it could be drink. Pilots are under a lot of pressure, with terrorists and everything.'

'People are very complicated.' Kyle was unsure what she meant by this but would not ask.

'Still, it makes one wonder,' he ventured. 'About gravity and all. If that had been a balloon and not a cow, we'd pay no attention.'

'Balloons are different.'

It was useless. Of course balloons were different. It was no surprise that the world was in disagreement about nearly everything. Humans fought like cats and dogs about trifles. Otherwise reasonable people were willing to be killed, and if necessary to kill, for causes none of them understood. Ditto political parties and, of course, nations, the most out of kilter entities of all. Kyle longed to let loose about all this. He wanted to hear how it would sound, wanted to get feedback. But Beth had no time for hypotheticals. She could talk forever about the children and now the grandchildren, or about the gossip that passed for conversation when her friends came to play cards. Just don't ask her to cope with an abstract thought.

'Ah, ice cream. My favourite.' It wasn't his favourite, apple tart was, but he needed to paddle back to the safe shallows of domesticity.

'Do you think the earth might be coming unglued, dear?' she asked casually as he transferred the dirty dishes to the kitchen.

'Beats me,' he suppressed his surprise. 'Why do you ask?'

'No reason at all.'

A few days later, as Kyle sat at his desk in the newsroom, the Pocket Oxford Dictionary rose into the air without obvious cause, hovered near the ceiling for a few moments, then slowly sank back until he could grab it. No one in the newsroom seemed to notice. He held it as if it were a foreign object, but it seemed to be the same book as always. He placed it on the desk, picked it up again. He wasn't used to this; no one was.

He went early to lunch, alone as usual. He needed to think. In addition to ordinary life there was magic. Then there were miracles. He had been reading up on everything, unsure through which door or window an insight might come. Miracles sometimes suspended the laws of nature. If, that is, one believed all that. Magic, in Kyle's estimation, was more iffy. Lastly, there was the human mind itself, which blew a fuse under certain circumstances.

But it wasn't just the mind, that shadowy faculty said to reside amid the lobes of the at-best mushy brain. The mind in turn relied on down-to-earth data. It saved one a lot of guessing and supposing if one could put one's hand on a book and feel it was real. Similarly, seeing and hearing and other faculties were priceless short cuts to whatever the average human needed to know.

Unless.

Doubt was one of the biggest, most obstinate words in any language.

Kyle had seen with his own eyes. On the other hand, the eyes sometimes fooled the mind. The world was full of fooled minds. Nature got glitches. Headaches, for example, were never part and parcel of the head, they were aberrations. Toothaches, too. Likewise, laws about houses staying put were, presumably, liable to exceptions.

For a journalist this raised added issues. The journalism world was full of slogans, such as *publish and be damned*, testimonies to human ambivalence. The ambiguity surrounding gravity wasn't yet widespread. What happened wasn't common, but if it could happen to a cow or a book, it could happen to anyone. The consequences were awesome.

'Did you hear about the bombing?' Beth asked. They had agreed not to watch television during dinner, a strategy to avoid becoming strangers.

'Which bombing was that?' he tried to sound interested.

'Probably the Middle East or one of those places.'

'You know whose fault that is…' Kyle said.

'It's not a question of fault.'

'And what is it?' Talking at dinner was a good idea, he had to grant Beth that much, but there were few topics they could agree on. Kyle had a theory that people got along better when they just grunted and gesticulated, the way we started out. Once language set in, it made possible too many areas of disagreement.

'Here's what I think.' Beth put down knife and fork as if she were about to deliver a long speech. 'What's missing is love.' She hesitated, as if she might say more, then picked up the knife and fork.

'How do you mean?'

'I don't know.' She was flustered. 'I don't know how to put it. Once upon a time there was love. And now it's gone.'

'You mean, like sex?'

'Of course not.' She pushed the spaghetti away. She was a computer technician. This vaguely defined occupation always left her at a loss when he asked about work. It seemed very focused and, as she liked to say, *recherché*, while Kyle's own brief at the newspaper was the great sweep of things. Thus the micro and macro often clashed at the dinner table, but this thing about love was a horse of a different hue. 'It's not the saturation coverage, Kyle, not the repressive regimes. There's that, but that's not it. Human nature has changed. People seem the same as before except that the love is gone.'

She came back to the subject every day for a week.

'It's as if the capacity for pity has been taken away.'

'But otherwise we're the same, you're saying?'

'I don't know. I don't notice anything else missing.'

'I don't know either,' Kyle said. It was great to be able to say one didn't know. Human ignorance was one of the few certainties left. 'I can only speak for myself, but I feel as much, you know, compassion as ever for, well, for people, for the unfortunate.'

'Me, too,' Beth said. 'There are still exceptions. It's a process.'

'This would be huge if we had a way to measure it.'

Kyle thought Beth was looking very well of late. The hairdresser had done wavy things with her hair. She was more interesting. She had set him thinking.

'About that cow the pilot saw,' she said out of the blue at the weekend. 'I think I know what's going on.'

'Really?' He was instantly alert.

'It's not just the cow, it's the whole universe, it's everything.'

'How do you mean?'

'The universe as we know it may be passé.' She had returned from the market and was putting away vegetables. 'Everyone says there are a hundred billion stars in our galaxy.'

'Do they indeed?'

'More or less. Astronomers say. And there are a hundred billion galaxies, they say. With moons and asteroids and black holes and what have you.' Kyle had often seen the fat books lying about but never dreamed she was delving so deeply into whatever it was—the universe presumably. Beth was a changed woman. 'We know all this because of progress,' she went on. 'It's only a few years since we thought the earth was flat, and look at us now. And you know what made the difference? Computers are the difference.'

She had a narrow mind fixated on the computer, he thought benevolently. Had she gone into plumbing instead, plastic pipes would be the difference.

'You've lost me,' he said, the simple truth.

'It's cyberspace, don't you see. A few years ago, cyberspace was empty, nothing there. But look at it now. Click a button and books are bought, rockets launched, movies made full of logical impossibilities that turn life as we know it upside down. All of a sudden we're living not only here but in outer space. Ordinary hackers are creating new universes every day. Soon we'll be able to simulate universes with self-conscious people in them. People who think for themselves, not like computer games that have to be programmed.' Kyle was astonished at the big interesting mind she had kept hidden for so long. 'People who make decisions.'

'In cyberspace?'

'Whatever you want to call it. Scholars call it the multiverse.'

'And what are they saying?'

'I don't know,' she said. 'I don't know where the computer leaves off and something else takes over. What if some civilisation we know nothing about has already made a better computer? If they can make little green people—we might as well call them people—who think for themselves, then they can just as easily simulate the laws of biochemistry. They call it simulating but it's really creation. The simulators wouldn't have to wait millions of years, as we did, for new creatures to evolve. All they would have to do is simulate computer supergeeks who could then programme their supercomputers to do the rest.'

When he went for a walk, a stone rose up from a heap of other stones in the park. It rose a few feet, then fell back. I should be afraid, Kyle thought. He looked around and there was no one. It was not a prankster. I need guts, he thought, and picked up the stone. It was a roundish rock, about as heavy as one would expect.

The following day, as he drove to work in his rusty Volkswagen, he saw a shiny red Honda win the war with gravity. It was already too high to tell whether it was occupied. He pulled over. Other vehicles were passing in a steady flow. He pointed at the car in the air, but it was at Kyle the drivers stared. He buttonholed an elderly pedestrian.

'Did you see that car?' He pointed at it.

'What car?' The old man scanned the sky.

'Eyes not too good?' Kyle suggested.

'My eyes are fine. It's your head needs fixin'.'

'All the same, there's a car up there.' Kyle drove on to work determined to tell his colleagues. All day he watched for clues of a conspiracy or some monumental joke. It was disorienting to observe the unseemly nonsense with which they filled the paper. Yet he didn't tell them, couldn't risk looking foolish.

At home, dinner was rushed because the girls were coming for bridge.

'Every six seconds someone dies of AIDS,' Beth said, applying Thousand Island dressing to the salad.

'Love wouldn't have saved them.' He guessed where she was going.

'Or it may be every six minutes. The world is changing.'

'You're damn right it's changing.' Frustration prowled around in his head and descended into his gut. 'I could tell you about change.'

'Oh?' But she wasn't paying attention.

'What about a car rising into the air?'

'It couldn't, Kyle. Cars don't do that.'

'I know they don't. But this one did.'

'Are you saying this actually happened?'

'A mile up the road.'

'You must be mistaken, dear.'

'And a stone. I saw a stone rise into the air.'

'Did you really?' Her tone switched from mild curiosity to mild concern.

'I really did.' He would be on record. He would save the floating house for a more opportune time. 'Do you know what I think?'

'What, dear?'

'Gravity is a thing of the past. Gravity has had it.'

'Could you put a match to the fire, Kyle.'

'You don't believe me.'

'Have you told anyone?' Her tone implied she hoped not.

Nero didn't fiddle while Rome burned. There were no fiddles. So Nero played bridge instead. Kyle retired to his office and warmed up the laptop. The central problem was credibility. Neither torture nor bribery had ever been able to force belief.

This was frustrating considering the outlandish things people did believe for no good reason.

Google coughed up untold references to gravitation. Kyle began with Wikipedia, fountain of knowledge for the amateur. Aristotle was mentioned at once—that man got credit for being the first to think of nearly everything. But he wasn't the only one. The Indian Brahmagupta explained in 628 of our era that 'bodies fall towards the earth as it is in the nature of the earth to attract bodies, just as it is in the nature of water to flow.' Not great, but it was probably news in 628. Then there was Newton, on whose head the apple allegedly fell, a wake-up call, who said: 'Every particle in the universe attracts every other particle with a force that is directly proportional to the square of the distance between them.'

This was no immediate help when someone's Honda had taken leave of what the poet called the surly bonds of earth. Newton seemed to say a thing had gravity the same way it had size. But along came Einstein, who mentioned spacetime, which only gives the impression that bodies have weight although they don't really. Kyle made notes whenever he thought he knew what they were talking about.

Beth always summoned him when the girls broke for tea. The Macki sisters were social activists and heaped vituperation on American president George W Bush.

'Einstein had a theory about spacetime,' Kyle tried to broaden the discussion.

'Einstein wouldn't have known Bush,' Debra said. 'Or is that how spacetime works?'

'On the subject of gravity,' Kyle persisted, 'if things have no weight in themselves, and if spacetime is as unpredictable as it sounds, then things here on earth, not to mention planets and whole galaxies, could begin to act, let's say, differently.'

'It's that Bush and his crowd,' Debra Macki fulminated. 'Can they be relied upon to stay in the orbits they're in?'

The penny dropped. Recent emotional turbulence in the mundane universe made sense, Kyle decided, only if some interloper were interfering with the status quo. It had to be a wily interloper, a resourceful interferer, because the status quo was a tough nut to crack. The only such agent Kyle could think of was the hacker mentioned by Beth in the simulation scenario. He decided to call it a hypothesis, namely that our world, somewhere back there, had become a cyberworld invented on a state-of-the-art computer by some advanced brain on a faraway planet whose citizens combined a sense of humour with a touch of cruelty. It would take heroic research to determine at what point our old world gave way to this new simulation. A smart hacker would have made the transition surreptitiously, would have eased us into the alternative nightmare where we would scarcely notice that we had left the Garden of Eden or whatever story explained us previously. A flying house was only a hiccup compared with bigger irregularities we had grown to take for granted, from Noah's Ark to world wars, from the dim-witted Bush to current celebrities who on closer inspection had bunions on their feet of clay.

Only gravity had held the thing together until now. Gravity couldn't be expected to do the impossible indefinitely.

'Let's get back to the cards,' Emily Macki, a gynecologist in real life, was saying.

Another few seconds and Kyle would have told them about stones rising into the air. That's how close I came to making a fool of myself, he reflected. The aim now is not to lose my head. Great minds can go soft in a jiffy if enough odd stuff pops up. Stray dilemmas buzzed about in his brain like midges at a picnic. Why was gravity the only *bête noir* while everything else seemed to chug along as usual? Why didn't the little green hacker let him run a three-minute or, better, a two-minute mile? Why didn't women, for a change, throw themselves at him? Of all potential aberrations, the gravity mix-up was the least inspired imaginable. Yet there was no higher authority to appeal to. If no further nonsense happens, he decided, I'll put it all behind me. I can't be accused of anything, not even negligence.

Later in the week, returning from the airport, he saw a woman rise slowly into the air. She was wearing jeans, that was how clearly he could see her, a robust woman, legs and arms spreadeagled. Kyle slammed on the brakes as traffic rushed by. He ran toward the spot. He shouted as he went. People looked at him but no one looked at the woman. Then she slowly sank back into somebody's garden, so slowly she might not be hurt.

'I made a beeline for the house behind which she descended,' he told Maurice Cadwell next day. 'A semi-detached yellow house. I tried the little gate, not wanting to waste time. In case she was hurt. Do you mind if I smoke?'

'Do you need to?'

'I haven't smoked for twenty years.'

'Have you a cigarette?'

'No. I thought, perhaps, you might.' He had found Cadwell in the directory. He had tried four other therapists, who could not fit him in sooner than a month. He told one of them that civilisation could be gone to outer space in a month. Cadwell promised him half an hour. Now it had stretched to two hours.

'You were trying to get into someone's garden?'

'The gate was locked, so I rang the doorbell. A petite housewife answered. I told her a hefty woman had dropped from the sky into her garden. She said I was mistaken. It's disconcerting that what sounds so rational can sometimes be so wrong. It's probably next door, she said—the dead body. No one mentioned a dead body, I reminded her.'

'And then?'

'So I went next door. Knocked on the big brass knocker, but there was no one home. I explored the back garden but found nothing. I went from door to door, the entire street, then the surrounding streets. If only I had found a body, I could have gone public. Dead or alive, she was the evidence I needed.'

'Evidence of what?'

'Am I really seeing it, do you think, doctor?'

'What do you think?'

Out on the street, the sun was cheerful, unusually bright. If the sun came any closer to earth, or vice versa, there would be damn little margin for error. People would be burned to cinders and the oceans would boil and bubble and there would be no one left to care or sound the alarm. He buckled himself into the old Volkswagen. He felt light, as if a breeze might blow him away. The Volkswagen, a vintage Beetle, felt fragile as tinfoil. He imagined a cosmic hacker playing idly with a keyboard, bored or inquisitive. Kyle, being a man, imagined the hacker was male, that was typical. The hacker was taking it easy: nothing extravagant like making a planet much less a multiverse; more down to earth in fact, if *in fact* any longer meant anything. He worried that the hacker might do a double-click on the gravity button. He realised he was sweating. The hacker in the sky had hit the sweat button. Then the panic button.

It was reassuring, when nothing terrible happened, to see how normal life was: traffic all snarled at rush hour and pedestrians putting one foot in front of the other in that fascinating way.

The devil we know, he knew, is better than the devil we don't. People too. People were streets ahead of any alternative he could think of. Exasperating at times, unreliable to a fault, nevertheless he could not imagine a hacker out there who was likely to improve on the average human.

'That thing you were talking about,' he said after he had washed the dishes, started a fire of aromatic logs, fixed two mugs of decaffeinated coffee. 'This isn't the same universe we started out in.'

'What do you mean?'

'It all started when I was at that conference and a house floated away.'

'You never mentioned it, dear.'

'An advanced civilisation could do it. Those billions of galaxies aren't there for nothing, just floating about. Something is going on. People, I suppose. Probably quite advanced. Imagine other civilisations experimenting with life for billions of years before we even came along. Once they made a virtual world, and gave virtual people free will, the rest was easy.'

'You're scaring me, Kyle. You sound like science fiction.'

'It's nothing to be scared of. There are no little green men. It's only us. We're the ones we've been waiting for, and writing the science fiction about, only we didn't recognise ourselves. Until now. Look at you, how you've changed.'

'You've changed too, dear. I was afraid to mention it in case the bubble might burst.' Her eyes, he noticed, had lost that desperate, haunted look. The glue she had been missing was returning, though he was loath to call it love as Beth did. 'Just look at you, you little green man,' her face danced with what looked suspiciously like joy, Beth who had laughed so little lately.

'See what I mean? You've changed. You're more amusing. Not to mention pretty.' Kyle grabbed her. Nearly a generation had passed since he'd tried anything so risqué.

'Oh, stop it, Kyle. Act your age.' But she gave him a big old kiss smack on the lips. After which one thing led to another.

Later, he went for a walk. He was profoundly relieved, almost walking on air. The scent of roses was coming from a garden. Birds flew. People were unworried and even laughing. His Volkswagen in the driveway was a reassuring sight. Even the flat tire was practically normal. Kyle sighed, a traditional human reaction to the real world. And thought: even if some sly trickster wanted to simulate a multiverse, he would never think of a Beetle.

Unless.

Writer-in-Residence

Think of this as a work of fiction. Any resemblance to real people, therefore, is purely coincidental. Otherwise they might sue. They live in a town everyone knows. It has a Tesco and Spar, Toyota and Fiat dealerships, flower shops and hairdressers with quaint names. There is a river and crumbling ruins and a round tower out the road. The locals play Gaelic and soccer but seldom win, due, it seems, to some vague lack of determination. The place nearly won the Tidy Towns on several recent occasions. In short, a fictional town.

Clarence arrived there on the train on a dark December night.

May met him at the station. She was big and buxom, there's one of her in every town, the conscience and instigator, keeping citizens on their toes. Christmas decorations conferred on the town a glitter daylight wouldn't even recognise. Strings of blinking bulbs reached from the Bank of Ireland across the street to the AIB in admirable harmony. A choir of three, possessed of a guitar but no drum, sang 'The Little Drummer Boy,' pa rum pa pum pum. Shoppers lugged shopping bags from Dunnes or Easons, unaware that Clarence had come among them.

'Years from now,' May was saying, 'we'll be able to boast that we gave you your start.' She was chair of the sub-committee set up by the county council to choose a writer-in-residence from the four applicants on her shortlist. 'That is, if we do give you your start.' Driving recklessly with one fat hand on the wheel of her Audi, she pointed out the church, the farmers' market, a chip shop where a drug dealer had killed another drug dealer the previous week. She double-parked outside the hotel and strode ahead of Clarence to the De Valera Room on the second floor where the three other sub-committee members waited amid an assortment of bottles. A tree in a pot in the corner was visibly wilting.

There is a pattern to civilisation. Once prosperity bought people their immediate needs and wants, minds turned to speculation: what now? This loose, unruly question always perplexed thinkers with time on their hands. The unexamined life is as old as the Greeks but the examined life is older. A tentative solution to this search for psychic ballast has, for some time, been writers-in-residence: unusual people invited someplace they don't belong to accept money to write about the locals or the Zeitgeist or about nothing at all. Once only a trend, this procedure has become the rage. Cities and towns boast writers-in-residence; cultural institutions likewise, from academic groves to the local creamery.

'It's not just writing,' said a maneen called Mylie, seventy or more, with a pointy chin just above where his chin should be. 'It's thinking things out.'

'No, that's philosophy,' said Mr Kerb, a grey eminence from his hair to his shoes, a building magnate whose houses would sell better in a town known to cherish culture. 'Consider the high kings of Ireland,' he said to Clarence, 'who always made room for a poet at the top table.'

'Poet my arse,' said Mylie, 'unless the poet in question was a sexually disposed female, and scantily clad at that. High kings didn't become high kings by being stupid.'

'What do you think yourself?' May asked Clarence, who was drinking a sober lemonade.

'There are thousands of towns, from Ur of the Chaldees to the stones and dead bones in your own county, buried in oblivion for one reason and one reason only—there was no writer-in-residence in place to immortalise whatever it was.' Clarence had found this in a book and learned it by heart.

The fourth member was a shy girl, Virginia, who asked: 'Are you more at home with fiction or non-fiction?'

'Oh, fiction, for sure.'

His great misfortune was to be left the farm by his father.

'I'm not cut out for farming,' he'd announced when he turned seventeen.

'Nor for much else,' his father looked up from the boiled egg. His mother put his clothes in a small suitcase with a view to England.

'Come home whenever you want,' the father said, with what sounded like remorse. Clarence would write letters home, and the mother would write back. Their topic was the old man pining away.

'Come home or he'll die.'

'If I come home he'll die,' Clarence replied. But he came. And the father died.

'If you're going to stay, you'd better find a wife,' the mother, a realist, said. This led to marriage to Brona, whom he met in the Mace market, a quiet girl, small. The father would have vetted her up and down and decided she'd be a poor breeder.

The mother died to make room for the new woman. If they were going to have children, Brona announced, they'd need to extend the house, make it over with big windows and curtains and an all-electric kitchen.

'It's an odd way to go about having children.' Clarence was droll. No one at school told him what irony was, but he saw it everywhere: a little cloud of humour floating about and pointing at people, who were, without exception, ridiculous.

Brona conceived the night after the new refrigerator was delivered. That's ironic for sure, Clarence's funny bone whispered in his ear. A beautiful daughter was followed a year later by another. Ambitious Brona transformed the old farmhouse. Under the plaster she discovered fine stone walls. Isn't that just like life, she would say to Clarence.

Gradually he found himself unable to get up in the mornings. He was physically fine. He was still a good eater, and Brona's cooking put his mother's memory in the shade. What was lacking was motivation, a word as vague as irony but when you came across it, you knew it.

Why? That was the issue. What was the point? It dawned on him that people must have been asking this question since the beginning of thinking, but the answers remained unclear. It surprised Clarence that people nevertheless carried on, looking the other way when it came to motivation. He found himself unable to do it.

Every morning, after hating himself for a while, he would read. Though his sojourn in England had been otherwise unproductive, it had brought him into contact with second-hand books. At first he didn't discriminate—his reading was dictated by the price of the book. He always knew about libraries but not until he was thirty-two did he venture in. All those novels were strumpets to seduce him.

He loved Brona. When the girls arrived he loved them too. When Brona eventually confronted him, he was full of remorse.

'I wasn't cut out for farming.'

'It's late in the day to find that out.'

'Come on to the pictures,' he'd say to soften her.

'After you move the cattle to the high field,' she would relent.

Cattle farming was lucrative as long as you fed the cattle. Clarence's cattle found themselves on a diminishing diet in a European Union where animals were coddled like children. Associated with the cattle coddling was endless work designed to keep the farm looking spiffy.

'Clarence,' Brona would whisper in the early days. Then the whispering turned to badgering. She talked less to Clarence, more to the two girls. Until, one morning, she had gone back to her mother, the note said. She did not ask for anything. She did not sound angry. He would have welcomed anger. Not that he thought he deserved it. He knew from his reading that his case was not unique. There were rotten scoundrels who abandoned nearest and dearest, but there were also decent people who did it. The more he read, the more he realised that writing was a tyrant. All artists were ruthless predators.

Not that Clarence was an artist. He was down to earth like a farmer. Six feet with, as the song said, some inches to spare; the big round shoulders and hairy arms seemed wasted in front of a book. There was a jut to his jaw that belied the lack of ferocity with which he confronted life. But once all that reading got a grip in any household, the traditional way of life was history. Imagination began to outweigh common sense.

He sold all the cattle. Then sent the money to Brona. Wrote remorseful letters. He never asked them to come back home—he could not promise them he'd get up in the mornings. He was sure Brona did not hate him. 'But if you do, a divorce is your best bet,' he wrote her. 'Your best years are ahead of you, and I, it seems, am behind you.'

The shine went off the electricals in the kitchen. It was hard to believe so much dust could gather in a house, coming, it seemed, out of nowhere. He read that most of the earth's dust was the discarded, pulverised dead skin of humans. He started making notes of such things. When he would get up, sometimes towards evening, his head would be full of the ideas he had read all day. To the notes he started adding new thoughts of his own, original ideas that had never before existed. He would survey the words and sentences, would rearrange them; he was rewriting before he even decided to write.

One cruel irony, he thought, was to look like a farmer without being one. This had worked for Patrick Kavanagh, but times had changed. He thought: denim, head to toe. He thought: a floppy hat, but with a plastic band under the chin, because he intended, when he got on his feet, to walk the fields. The denims required money. He sold the high field, which lay alone beyond the river, an orphan. Clarence remained on good terms with the neighbours, who never mentioned the empty fields that would be knee-deep in grass come spring. Once one slowed down and allowed irony to penetrate, a more reasonable world came into focus. The spring would take care of itself, even tomorrow would. He had news for naysayers should he come across any: each life needed a fresh story and no one else could write yours for you.

Facts of life heretofore ignored became important. One was the writers' group that met once a week in the snug at Gilligan's. He wandered in on a Monday evening.

'Have you taken up the pen, Clarence?'

'Aye, I was thinking about it.'

'Good man, good man.' He liked the way they encouraged him and each other. One read a short story; another a chapter of what she called creative non-fiction; several read poems. Clarence, enthused, joined in the low-octane critique.

'Have you anything yourself?' they then asked.

'I'm working up to it.' Their offerings ranged from serious to depressing. He might, for a change, let irony creep in through the cracks.

The next morning was an eye-opener. Sleep abandoned him. The sun came up fresh and demanding. Clarence reached for a yellow pencil. Writing was easy. All you needed was words, and no need for jawbreakers or showing off. Get the important things down. Emotions and that. There would be decisions to make. Punctuation would be a killer: he was never good at commas.

He was up by noon, hours ahead of himself. He couldn't wait to make sentences, as if he hadn't been doing it all his life. He had bought a computer when he sold the field. It whirred all day and into the night.

The next day, he was up with the sun. Life had a purpose.

The following Wednesday he read a long piece about the South Pole and the intrepid explorers who risked everything to go there.

'Good man yourself,' the others were enthusiastic, a dozen of them, mostly women, getting their pensions now. No one said he was ready for the Nobel Prize, but no one said he wasn't. 'You should write about what you know,' one said bluntly. 'Write about yourself.' He didn't tell them he knew the South Pole better than he knew himself. That was where the irony came in.

Once destiny gets started, it doesn't know when to stop. Clarence saw, in the arty page of the local paper, that a certain town far away needed a writer-in-residence. The further away the better, he thought. He was not surprised eventually to find himself on the shortlist because a logical inevitability was coming to pass.

Experts can tell you there is a bureaucracy for running things since art became lucrative and sculptors and scribblers came out of obscurity to limn the soul of a new, improved nation. This process is complicated and has been accused of strangling imagination. The Muse, they say, now has a degree in art management instead of art.

Since this is fiction, though, the local committee, instead of bringing an expert down from the city, opted to make up its own mind. It embarked on another bottle of wine.

'Fiction is fine,' Mylie was in his shirtsleeves and the red tie askew like a hangman's knot, 'but between you and me, fiction is no match for what actually happened.' He was the local historian, he'd said several times.

'But what actually happened?' Clarence asked innocently. 'That's the thing.'

'I know it's the thing,' Mylie conceded. 'Did you ever hear about the UFO that came our way, back in fifty-eight, or was it fifty-seven, no, what am I saying, it was fifty-eight?'

'A UFO from outer space, do you mean?'

'Where else would it come from?'

'And where did it land?'

'Land? Are you out of your mind? No now, it came motoring

down. There are only a few of us left who remember that historic day. Towards evening, it was. Around milking time—I can still remember the mournful lowing of the cows, as well as the thrushes, do you see, like they knew something was afoot, it was that class of an evening. Not a cloud in the sky, as if they had been cleared out in advance of the thing—some of us thought the pilot might have been blinded by the sun. What a noise. What a catastrophe.' The De Valera Room fell silent.

'And did you see them?'

'Who?'

'The little fellows in the UFO?' Nothing in his background had prepared Clarence to frame the question. 'The extraterrestrials?'

'Are you out of your mind? All we ever saw was a hole in the ground. The smart money said they kept on going and came out on the other side, down by Australia, it would be no bother to them with their amazing brand of technology.' Mylie looked from face to face. The others were running out of awe, but that did not make the story less true. He would drink half the pint at a time, Mylie, with a gurgling sound as the porter passed his adam's apple. Yet he never once went to the toilet, which in its own quiet way was as big a wonder as the UFO.

At approximately this time, Clarence, while he was away on a visit to the loo, was appointed writer-in-residence by unanimous vote after a quick confab. In any genre but fiction there would be awkward questions to answer here. Such as what happened to the other three writers on the shortlist. Or why the sub-committee entrusted to such an untried rustic the reputation of a contemporary town.

The truth is, fiction is quite like reality, which is hard-nosed and wants to get on with things. Mr Kerb, May said to Clarence when he returned from the toilet, would be funding the venture in lieu of the county council or anyone else who might insist on strings attached. The stipend, furthermore, would be doubled, enough to pay the piper for a whole year.

'What do you want me to write?' Clarence was unsure how

any of this worked.

'Write whatever you want,' Kerb combined the self-assurance of the filthy rich with the benevolence of medieval monarchs eager to elevate impoverished minds struggling out of the dark ages. 'We hope you'll leave our town a better place, that's all.'

'I will, I will,' Clarence said earnestly.

'You'll need to get out and talk to people,' May admonished. 'Get their life stories, their hopes, their bunions.' She had taken on a lot of red wine. 'You'll find they're mostly hypocrites. Thieves, half of them. The dirt. Get the dirt. Oh, I envy you, Clarence.'

'And don't forget that murder in the quarry,' Mylie added. 'In 1939, or was it 1938?'

'It must have been 1939 because Hitler was at—it must have been the big war he was at. Would you try a whiskey, Clarence? You'll think better.'

'Aye, and write better.'

'Cox, it was,' Mylie wagged his feisty little chin. 'Felled his neighbour, Wallace, with a hatchet.'

'I think it was vice versa,' May said with a hiccup.

'What was it about?' Though unsure how to be writer-in-residence, Clarence knew he needed some demeanour, an attitude. He needed to be quizzical yet aloof. He thought of Graham Greene in his trench coat—though it wasn't the coat, it was something more psychological, formidable yet devil-may-care. There were never any gods on Mount Olympus; people had put gods there so that they could then look up to them. Despite being ridiculous, people were smart. He realised there was a lot of thinking to be done. Sophistication, if he could harness it, would come in handy. He might, ultimately, need to try whiskey.

'About?' May was saying. 'It was about a woman. Whatever about Cox, Wallace killed for love.'

'And vice versa,' Mylie was sinking slowly into a historical fog in which ancestors were ghosts inspired by mythical causes. 'Along these country roads there isn't a mile in any direction where someone didn't die for Ireland.'

Bashful Virginia, auburn hair reaching far down her back, sat upright with her orange drink. She's here because she's the future, Clarence decided; she'll require special attention like the high kings gave the naked poets.

'A few words about my new development wouldn't hurt,' Kerb stood tall and important in front of the gas fire.

'Oh aye,' Mylie confirmed, 'and don't forget Mr Kerb's mall. Grander than a cathedral, that place. We're richer now, Clarence, than the saints and scholars ever suspected we'd be.' It sounded like praise but there was an undertone. Clarence would need to watch for undertones.

'Then there's the castle,' May announced. 'You'll be sleeping in the same bed as the Earl of—what was that earl, Mylie?'

'Now there's some dispute about that earl.'

'Ah fuck it, Mylie, don't start that again.'

'It's your castle, Mr Kerb, no two ways about it.'

'Exactly. Here,' Kerb handed over a monumental, rusty key. 'Treat that national treasure with respect. There are memories of dead people there, though they're too long gone to be ghosts.' Clarence felt euphoric when he realised there was so much more to Irish capitalism than dog-eat-dog.

'There never was a poorer poorhouse than ours,' Mylie was still talking to the night after the others had left. Virginia was detailed to take Clarence to his castle. A moon floated above the Christmas decorations. The choir had gone home but the melody lingered.

In the small hours of the morning, the castle walls made sinister shapes. Water from a lake sulked in the black shadows. Clarence, still cold sober, saw the Earl at an upper window.

'It's only rubble,' Virginia said.

'It's first class rubble. There's no roof, or am I imagining it?'

'Kerb is going to make a luxury hotel.' One room, however, had already been refurbished. 'The scriptorium,' she called it. There was a bed and a refrigerator and a microwave, 'and in there is the place when you need, you know, to go.'

He waved goodbye to Virginia, an understated wave like the Earl's. He lit a fire in the sprawling fireplace of the scriptorium, then fell asleep on black bricks the long-dead ancestors had put there. Clarence saw them at it. He had arrived at a place where the real and imagined blended, and this epiphany derived, he knew, from being writer-in-residence. The ancestors that he saw had bad teeth and one had only one eye, and fights would break out, which was how the one eye came about. Yet, slowly, they put the brick floor in place, a practically everlasting floor if left undisturbed by the barbarian Kerb.

In the pocket of his country topcoat was a fat envelope deposited by May, including a wad of money from Kerb, and a contract specifying that he needn't write if he didn't want to. I won't let them down, Clarence said to himself before falling asleep. He had stumbled on an outlandish stroke of luck. Including dodging miles of red tape. The bureaucrats would have made him do the writing first to prove he deserved the money to do the writing.

By broad daylight not much had changed. There were people everywhere, all dead. The castle was full of souls, as were the gardens and fields. He saw children playing and women working. It wasn't all harmony. A body with outflung limbs was occasionally thrown from a high window into the lake. A writer-in-residence had many options. He could romanticise it all; he could praise the good and make excuses for the dubious in a hodgepodge of ethical stirabout; he could pack up and go home.

He had no idea what other writers-in-residence did. He suspected some got away with nonsense about the lark in the clear air. It was a problem being oneself, in his case an ignorant farmer. He had learned lots of things from books but there would always be a lack. A lack of common sense, for one thing. Moments when he wasn't exuberant, he would remember the homestead deserted and the family dispersed. He wrote to

Brona. He didn't say he loved her because any day now she might file for divorce and he didn't wish to complicate her life. He then wrote to the darling daughters and said, yes, he loved them fiercely.

The castle had a toaster. The Earl would have killed for a toaster. Or for the imported marmalade with foreign descriptions in three languages. Breakfast was followed by a bowel movement in the gleaming toilet. He was not in the least embarrassed— even poets laureate did it—but he wouldn't write about shite as some writers loved to do. He circled the town, getting the lie of the land. When he ran out of roads and boreens, he took to the fields, crossing walls of loose stones, crawling under electric fences, saying an odd word to farm animals in a language that was neither his nor theirs.

'God bless the work,' he greeted a farmer stringing up barbed wire.

'Are you lost or something?' the farmer asked.

'No loss on me.' A laughing dog stood by the farmer, a dog that could bite your behind in a minute because dogs were suspiciously like people.

Eventually the walking took him into town, up and down every street in search of the unpredictable. He stopped in a sandwich place for a snack. People were naturally curious. A soft talker for a big man, he replied modestly that writing was his calling and he would like to ask them about the town, including themselves.

'Why would we bother?' was the frequent reaction.

'For posterity, I suppose. That way you won't have lived without being noticed.'

'You'll write it down?'

'Oh for sure.' This alarmed some and pleased others. Several invited him into pubs for a pint. 'All right, so.' Lemonade would never get the job done. Millions had been drinking porter for centuries, people and porter were a match, each a boon to the other.

By dusk he was drunk as a lord. My first day on the job and look at the change in me, he said to the locals with a lisp he had never noticed before. Life is ironic, he told them in reply to every awkward question, 'and when I sober up I'll write about ye all.' A dozen of them surrounded him on wooden benches, hanging on his words, and he fleetingly regretted all the days he had wasted sleeping.

'What can ye tell me about the UFO beyond?'

So they went out the road in vans, soon after midnight, in search of the legendary aliens. Each one remembered the thing in a different field or down a different lane. Squabbles arose. A farmer appeared out of the darkness with a spade and threatened to decapitate anyone who stepped on his grass. The story was already forming in Clarence's head. It wouldn't be fiction; it would be epic fiction.

Days passed. Clarence climbed to the turret of his castle each morning and observed old battles won and lost. He observed evictions, and long-dead blue bloods chasing maidens through thickets and into cow byres whence shrieks of passion would soon emanate.

Virginia arrived in her small car wearing what looked like a see-through dress. 'You're looking well,' he told her.

'If I can be of any help?'

'It's a good thing this is fiction,' Clarence said. 'Otherwise I wouldn't know what to do.'

'Well, now you know.'

When they finally awoke in Clarence's narrow bed, it seemed to be twilight. Birds were singing.

'Do you know what I think?' Clarence said. 'I think this is not how the writer-in-residence thing works. This is the twenty-first century, and everyone is sophisticated and has gone to see the world in Prague or New York or at least Cork, and people with laptops keep track of the whole caboodle, they'd know better than to let loose a moron like me to chronicle the living never mind the dead of this town. They'd want people with degrees and diplomas, extroverts and social networkers and cool dressers.'

'If there was a formula for writers-in-residence,' she said, 'that would defeat the whole purpose.'

'Would you like to see the castle?'

'They were all mad, the earls. Those were the days when the English sent their mentally handicapped over here to keep an eye on the Irish.'

Soon after Virginia left, Mr Kerb drove up in his Land Rover.

'Don't let the past beguile you,' he cautioned. 'Look unflinchingly at the future. Then tell me how do you see this heap of stones in, say, another thousand years?'

In response, Clarence told him how he had deposited his stipend for safe keeping behind a loose stone in the castle wall. But there were so many loose stones he could no longer locate the money.

No letter came back from Brona, not even a phone call.

'The more I yearn, the more I don't know what for,' he confided to May—the entire sub-committee was keeping an eye on its investment.

'Tell us about her,' May, kind for a curmudgeon, encouraged him.

'You have me now. I never paid much attention, and when she was gone it was too late.'

'What colour was her hair?'

'Hard to say. She was a toe short on her left foot, I remember that.' But he couldn't see her face, not plainly. She had gone leaving no photos behind, neither of herself nor the children. And anyway, last year's faces would be different now.

'Would you say she was pretty?'

'Oh she was. Pretty alright.' He searched his memory. She must have laughed when she still loved him. She surely had a small soft hand before the farm hardened it. He remembered her wide backside, unless it was someone else's. In the days that followed he would sometimes glimpse her face, then it would be gone wherever memory hid it.

The townspeople brought bags of turf when they learned what Clarence was up to, namely art. Not since the Earl succumbed had such fires flourished, making shadows on pillars and lumpy walls. He sat on a wooden stool and wrote codswallop.

Write what you know, they used to say at the writers' group. But how was a writer to know what he knew? He wrote about the UFO until it became unreal and no longer existed. Mylie told him yarns about a dead hangman between the wars and about the shenanigans of the LDF during the Emergency. He wrote about a local saint who had a stained-glass window in the church in Church Street, until Mylie informed him the saint had been discontinued in a Vatican purge. That's ironic for sure, Clarence mused, but not a bit funny. Each time he ran out of ideas he would hear the drummer boy, pa rum pa pum pum on his drum. It's not memory remembers, he'd then say to himself, it's imagination.

He arose every morning at dawn. He wrote to Brona that getting up was no longer a problem.

He read in a book that what you look at hard enough will look back at you. The more he wrote about Brona, the more she looked back at him. Gradually he brought her to life until she eventually talked to him—she and the babies, whose names were Una and Ebana, were gone a year and more.

Then a letter came. It was battered and smudged front and back with post office stamps and scribbles—try such a place, the scribbles said as the letter travelled throughout Ireland in search of Clarence. He left it under a rafter in the castle for two days while he prepared mentally for what it might say. He walked the streets. He walked the fields, overwhelmed by all he didn't know, especially people's secrets. He climbed the little dunghill of a mountain for perspective, a God's eye view. The town remained unclear as the misty weather.

'Did you read the letter?' the postman asked, because the town knew more about Clarence than he knew about the town.

'First thing tomorrow, I'll do it.'

Brona's was a short letter. 'In case you never receive it,' she explained. 'The little girls are fine, and so am I.'

How could they be fine? Hadn't their father taken to sleeping all day? When it came to letters, so much was written between the lines. The more he read, the more pain he found there: loneliness and hopelessness. This was never blurted out because that wouldn't be Brona, who was gentle, not a mean bone in her body. Clarence found himself slipping into a hell where the memories were pitchforks torturing him.

He talked to his mentors: May and Mylie and Virginia and Mr Kerb. They had great power, he reminded them. When they provided opportunities for writers, they would need to be careful. Art was fierce wild, it didn't obey rules, it didn't show mercy, didn't do favours.

'Sure all we did was give you money,' Mylie's eyebrows refused to sit still.

'That's not all,' May corrected. 'We gave him ideas. Especially about himself.'

'I'll write to her,' Clarence promised, and the emergency meeting broke up.

'I remember you well,' he wrote to Brona. 'I remember you on the tractor and around the house hanging curtains and frying rashers and black pudding. You were always jolly and you singing Elvis Presley songs.'

'I never sang E. Presley songs,' she wrote back, 'and as for curtains, you wouldn't let me have the money.'

Fiction was easier. It didn't talk back.

He wrote to her about the babies once so small he held one in the palm of each hand. 'You fitted into this world better than me,' he wrote. 'I was always a misfit.' Yet he didn't give in to her on everything. 'Don't think it's easy lying in bed when you don't know what else to do. Don't think there's no pain.'

He would eat potatoes baked in the castle microwave and

lathered with butter. Sometimes Virginia would visit him with vegetables and ice cream.

He looked up *delirious* in the dictionary. It was, as he suspected, neither all bad nor all good.

When December came around, May drove him to the train station. He was sad leaving that mysterious town. People waved to him and he waved back. He had been the only writer-in-residence they had ever known. He had spied on them, chatted and confided, eating and drinking with them and hoping for something to turn up. He had done them favours they didn't realise, such as an embellished history and brighter prospects coming soon. In some small way he had lifted them up, given them hope. He had discovered Mylie's UFO under a bush. He had found blue skies for the town, and a taller, more purple mountain, so that people bought Kerb's houses each of which had gold fixtures inside and cuckoos outside. The Earl made a comeback, nobler than before; no more rack rent but pomp and processions for tourists.

In the square the little shivering choir was back singing:

> I played my best for Him,
> Then He smiled at me,
> Me and my drum.

'It's a pity you didn't get the dirt on half of them,' May was saying, 'especially the liars and fornicators. This town is full of them.'

'Love is better than the other,' Clarence replied. 'Come rain or shine, love is nimble and your best bet.' Since buying the dictionary he had learned a way with words. May, won over, smiled, pa rum pa pum pum.

The train took him within walking distance of the old homestead. He walked under outstretched bare branches of ancient ash and sycamore. Fields by the road were waiting for new cattle. The house needed work. Weeds had been thriving and were resting for the winter. Windowpanes had been broken by vandals. Clarence, too excited to sleep, worked day and night until the house was a marvel. The transformation was finished just in time for Brona and the girls arriving happy and waving.

All this was in the novel.

Pascal's Wager

Every morning, out of the blackness, a hint of brightness would appear, impossible to say when one gave way to the other. Soon a saffron ribbon would emerge, or some silver lining, or, on days of destiny, bronze. After that it was only a matter of time until the world was up and making mischief.

Ronan looked at his watch. Not yet seven. His pyjamas sported a white crossways stripe like a jailbird. His large angular head hinted at a big bony body under the blankets. The chemo had taken the little hair that was left at eighty. The blue eyes were alert like lights on a dashboard that showed the motor still running.

'Good morning, Malachy,' he said when the watch edged past seven. Ronan had volunteered to double up with Malachy, who had not spoken a word for two years. 'Another foggy one, I'm afraid. Did you sleep well?' He always threw in a question in case a miracle happened overnight and Malachy might be bursting to talk.

Down the hill past the two ash trees was the river—which was why this was called the Riverside Nursing Home—a prudent river that never overflowed. Where it took a turn one could see the water reflecting the bronze sky. The wall was still there, if it was a wall. And where the wall met the water: a boat, if it was a boat.

Someone shuffled by on the corridor. From the distance came

the clatter of dishes. 'I'll will you all my worldly goods, Malachy, if you'll just say something.' Ronan scratched his groin. He could stand himself no longer, reached for the mobile.

'I need to urinate.' He knew Starski was on duty.

'Good morning, Ronan,' she said affably. 'You know how to urinate. Or shall I walk you through it, step by step?'

'If you would, please.' But she had cut him off. He eased himself out of bed, sat for a minute to check aches and pains. He had only one crutch, which he used under the right or left wing depending on the spur of the moment. 'I'll be back in a minute, Malachy, don't go anywhere.'

When he emerged from the toilet he got into the faded blue robe. The television set was still asleep on the wall. The wardrobe had a mirror attached, in which the remaining tatters of his ego refused to look at him. On the locker beside his bed was a black-faced clock, a stack of books and more on the floor. Malachy's side of the room was crowded with medical instruments and plastic tubes, one of which was stuck in his nose supplying a sort of life. There was a print of a clamp of wet turf by Paul Henry on one green wall and a calendar on another. It was a hard room to love. He phoned Starski: 'The senior occupant of 244 is moving out. Malachy wishes to be excused.'

'Leave me alone, Ronan,' Starski said. He never risked phoning the other nurses.

In the dining room, Benny and Sara were already eating their bran flakes.

'You're late,' Sara said. She was ninety and counting. She had lost her dentures years ago and no one had ever replaced them. She was in love with Ronan and told him so whenever she could pry him loose from Benny, who in turn was in love with Sara. The three of them stuck together, Benny said, because they were the only intellectuals left in the nursing home.

'The sun came up again,' Ronan announced as he attacked his lukewarm porridge.

'It's tireless, that sun,' Benny said. 'That's several times this week.'

'You're looking debonair, Ronan,' Sara said, 'you must have slept a sight.' She had spilled the milk and it dripped from the table into her lap.

'Thank you, Sara.'

Meanwhile, other residents were wheeled into the dining room. The walls were green like the bedrooms and kissed in places by the sun. The toast arrived. One girl brought coffee and another tea. Life seemed ordinary, Ronan thought, yet every time the sun showed up it instigated enough intrigue to drive the world out of its mind. He pulled out the mobile and dialled expertly with his thumb.

'This is Ronan O'Day, don't hang up. I need to go to confession… I know—I'm sorry, I won't do it again.'

'What did he say?' Benny wanted to know.

'He didn't say anything, he just hung up.'

'By the hokey,' Benny's laugh sounded like a series of hiccups. He wore stylish, gold-rimmed glasses and never left his room except in his blue striped suit and a white straw hat on his round head. 'If I was you I'd report him to the bishop.'

'It's no use. The bishop is running out of clergy and the few who are left have forgotten how to hear confessions.'

'Sure, don't I know. I never bother myself.'

'You're looking debonair, Ronan,' Sara returned to her theme.

'Did I ever tell you about Pascal's Wager?' Ronan asked.

'Tell it, Ronan,' Sara coaxed.

'Just between ourselves, Pascal's Wager is why I need confession.'

'Go on,' Benny encouraged.

'Do you believe in God, Benny?'

'Well sure I do.'

'And have you any proof?'

'I don't need any—haven't I got along grand without proof until now?'

'A God that might send you to hell?'

'Oh, I'm going to hell for sure,' Sara said with enthusiasm.

'Blaise Pascal,' Ronan held up the cup for more coffee and dumped an extra spoonful of sugar into it, feeling expansive, an intellectual among intellectuals. A world of nostalgia drifted up from his days at university when athletic young men and mysterious girls solved ancient enigmas in cafés down Dublin's side streets on evenings that had no end. 'Blaise Pascal was a philosopher, you see.'

'A what?' Sara asked.

'One can't be sure God exists: that's where Pascal came into the picture. Aquinas's five proofs, Anselm's ontological argument, when it comes to real life these are only old wives' tales.' He lit a cigarette. 'Here's the nub of it: God either exists or doesn't exist. If the chances are fifty-fifty, you might be tempted to take a sporting chance. But you'd be on thin ice. Because, if you backed the wrong horse, hell might be waiting on the other side.'

'You're a genius, Ronan,' Sara's head was lolling, her eyelids drooping.

'So if one met God over yonder, with heaven in his right hand and hell in the left, a hell full of burning and regretting that might go on for eternity, one could, to say the least, be in a fix.'

'So long as there's a toilet there, I won't mind,' Benny said and shuffled off.

'But if one has wagered on God's majestic existence,' Ronan focused his full attention on the sleeping Sara, 'then one can face the future with equanimity. If, at the heel of the hunt, we find no one there, we won't have lost anything. We'll just have darkness, which, under the circumstances, won't bother us. But if God is indeed among those present, why, we'll be glad we bet on a winner. That's what Pascal said, back when the world was innocent.'

Sara opened one eye and smiled.

'But there's a catch, Sara, old doll. If we bet on God, we have to stick with the straight and narrow. Don't bear false witness. Put money in the poor box. Go to confession when lust raises its head or we want to kill a neighbour.'

Several crows were perched in the trees beyond the window,

sullen and watching. Another couple arrived and a few flew off. They knew a lot from observing people. Certain crows were said to live ten thousand years, and the last thing the world needed was some ornithologist to come along and disprove this for her Master's thesis. Ronan removed the mobile from his robe pocket, put the robe around Sara's shoulders.

'Spiffy pyjamas, Ronan,' Starski passed him on the corridor.

It took an hour to dress. 'It's not us, Malachy, it's time that has shrunk since we were young.' He dialled again. 'Is that Riverside Radio?…This is Ronan O'Day, don't hang up. Aye, the schoolmaster. Am I on the air?… The priest refuses to hear my confession…Very well, I'll be back tomorrow.'

The carers had changed Malachy's sheets during breakfast. They had topped up the liquid in his plastic pouch. Short of a miracle, he would never eat another fried egg. His closed eyes pretended to peer over the fresh white linen. He didn't need to be conscious for his hair to keep growing, and his white stubble. Occasionally there would be an accident under the sheets followed by the odour of sanctity, which the carers took in their stride because they all had hearts of gold.

'Hold the fort, old friend.' He took two extra pills for the pain. He buttoned up the topcoat and slipped out the side door. When the sun came from behind a gable, his pale shadow hobbled ahead of him down the hill. All he could see was a dab of colour in the distance. The only excuse to call it a boat was its proximity to the river. That, and a belief in destiny. The bladder was a problem, unpredictable and impatient. When he reached the hedge, he peed with satisfaction on the safe side of the laurels.

A moment came when the coloured object was unmistakably a boat. That still left unanswered questions. Was she seaworthy? Were there oars? Still, one had to take some risks with life.

'It's a boat alright,' he announced to Sara and Benny at teatime. 'You know the routine,' he said to Benny after Sara fell asleep by the radiator. Benny grinned until his face bulged, and saluted in silence.

Back in his room, Ronan phoned again. 'I need confession,' he said without preamble.

'The last time,' the priest said, 'you blasphemed.'

'And if you come over, I'll confess it.' The lonely purr of the phone told him the priest had hung up. 'Did you hear that?' Ronan said to Malachy. 'You'll have to do.'

He brushed his teeth. He turned the bedside light low, lay on his back on the bed.

'It's sixty years, more or less, since my last confession.' He lit a cigarette, placed the ash tray on his belly, blew slow smoke at the ceiling.

'If it's all right with you, we'll skip the preliminaries and go straight to the meat and potatoes.' He glanced at Malachy, who raised no objection. 'There was a girl—that's the part I want to get at. When I was at the university. We were all young—young and foolish, what can I say, but in fairness we were also planning to change the world. Debating about Plato and Nietzsche and Moses and the pope, drinking and smoking and showing off.

'There was one girl, as I say.' How explicit would he need to be? A real priest would probe for the telling little details. 'Everyone said how beautiful she was. I took their word for it, though personally I don't any longer see that it mattered. When word spread that she was pregnant, Nietzsche proved to be of little help. There were no potential fathers rushing forward to claim their prerogatives. And there was no wronged high-cheeked girl to point the finger. She had disappeared. It was easy to disappear because none of us looked very far. The summer exams were approaching. We had futures to think about. We hid behind our books until the storm blew over. Not a storm, either—she could have created one, but only a gentle breeze blew through the space she had occupied in our lives. Word spread that her family had disowned her; that she was working with the nuns in a laundry in the south. No one accused anyone of hardheartedness, much less of fathering the baby. If there ever was a baby. One morning, it was as if none of us had ever met her or each other. On one ordinary day we became strangers created by this disappeared girl. We walked past each other in silence, taking short cuts to the rest of our lives.

'After the exams I would search for her, I vowed. I would rescue her from that laundry. I would cherish her and marry her just as soon as I found time and got my life in order. If there were a child I would be her father, or his father, even if she didn't look a bit like me. Then one thing led to another, and I started teaching, and I never got my life sufficiently in order to go and find her. I was waiting to have a bit of money, a better job. Above all I was waiting for the backbone to claim a daughter or son already two years old and then three, then ten or twenty. Every year the undertaking grew more formidable. I steered clear of marriage, because if such an occasion arose, I would be forced to search first for the other woman. In the end I felt we were married, wherever she was. An unwritten contract bound us together. I was convinced she had not married either. We were both waiting for the right moment when our lives would finally be in order.'

He threw a glance at Malachy and waited. He didn't expect the usual absolution—that came from a higher authority. But this would be a good time for a few words. Malachy, however, held his peace.

'I'll say one Our Father and ten Hail Marys so,' Ronan said. 'That should cover it.' He prayed them silently, meticulously, as the cautious Pascal would have done. Beyond the window, half a moon was leaning over. It would be throwing light on the boat. Ronan put on the topcoat and tightened the belt buckle. He put on the woollen cap and scarf. He put his wallet in one pocket and toothbrush in the other, picked up the flash lamp, and carried the crutch under his arm, that way it would make less noise.

'Thanks for everything, old pal,' he tweaked Malachy's toe.

He knocked discreetly on Benny's door. Benny wore a large puffy jacket like a tent, and an orange scarf across his lower face like a bandit.

'It's very mysterious, Ronan,' Benny said as they stumbled and slithered down the hill towards the river.

'There's a woman lives on the other side.' He had to tell Benny something.

'Aren't you the sly devil.'

'Keep it quiet, Benny, or Starski will come after us.' They stopped to pee behind the laurel hedge, then they pushed on. She might be on the other side—it was a mighty big world over there. If she ever existed. That would have been the year he was twenty-two. But he couldn't remember being twenty-two.

'Do you remember 1942, Benny?'

'Can't say I do.'

'Me neither.' Ronan felt relieved. That year had never taken place. Sometime he'd search for old calendars or newspapers just to make sure.

'Slow down,' Benny said, falling behind.

On the other hand, there was, according to some, the golden book. What mattered was whether the recording angel remembered the year in question. Pascal's Wager was more than an intellectual exercise. To be quite frank about it, a man with an immortal soul needed to cover his arse.

He looked back at Benny sitting on a stone.

'Take this, Benny,' he handed over the flash lamp. 'If you go back now, you'll be in time for the bran flakes.'

'Goodbye so, Ronan.' Benny's soul had a shorter wing span. They shook hands solemnly.

The moon pointed a finger at the boat. The boat tensed and held together. Ronan unwrapped the chain from around a stone. He shook off old age and infirmity and gave her a push, then a pull, up to his ankles in the dirty water. She moved readily enough, went with him, until it seemed she was pulling him along. There was an oar and then another, stretched patiently across the two seats. Only then did he realise that the boat had been waiting there, year after year, for some codger from the nursing home to grab the bull by the horns and give destiny a last chance. He threw his leg over the side as once on summer days. Pushed with the oar in the rushes. Settled himself on the cold seat. Eased the boat out into the dark water where the silver half-moon danced. And headed for the future.

Up in the nursing home, a few lights had refused to go out. He pulled out the mobile.

'Starski? There you are.'

'I'll kill you, Ronan,' she was affable as ever.

'Benny is safe and sitting on a rock. He'll be home in time for breakfast.'

Before she could respond, he threw the mobile in the water.

Dandelion

Margaret was a farmer's wife until the farmer died. She then sold the farm for more money than the late Hughie had ever imagined. The first thing she bought was a computer. There were no children; there was only a sister in Seattle. Margaret, already seventy-eight, chuckled and cackled and randomly plied the keyboard until, early in March, contact was made.

The sister was delighted. She emailed Margaret long screeds about life in the Northwest. Margaret sent screeds of her own about events in the village. They soon had said everything that needed to be said and grew bored with one another. By the end of March, Margaret's computer was gathering dust.

Life got lonely. Belatedly she grieved for Hughie. Then she grieved for herself. She thought about eternity and its implications. On a Saturday morning she grabbed a handful of money and took it to the priest to offer a Mass.

'I hear you got a computer, Margaret,' the priest said.

A dandelion looked up from the grass as he shuffled from his house to the church. Father Killian O'Loan, without realising it, was a mystic. Even the most despised flower could get him going. It couldn't be just earth, he thought. If you looked up and had fierce eyesight, you'd see a billion heavenly bodies in one square foot of sky. If the law of averages meant anything, there must be at least one dandelion out there somewhere. But the law of averages was a cod when everyone demanded proof. Faith, once an extraterrestrial ally, had grown feeble some years earlier, back around the time of the Rolling Stones, and with each passing year it was harder to make the leap.

The sandstone church was hunkered down behind evergreen trees. A round window stared across the parish. It had waited a century for stained glass, but by the time parishioners could afford the stained glass they had become avid materialists and had lost their supernatural drive. A spire pointed at the blue sky, a white cross on top. You wouldn't find that in any other galaxy. Molecules and nuclei and sticks and stones could never come together like that by coincidence. It took superhuman imagination to think up entirely new things that had neither previous names nor history.

Killian had not dressed like a priest for twenty years. He wore the same old sweaters for confessions as he wore for golf on Tuesdays. At seventy-four he was still trim, a bantamweight. He had pink cheeks that on closer inspection were decorated with tiny veins, handwriting of the years.

There were four cars parked by the road. Once, the car park would be crowded and frantic, so that souls fresh from confession would lose their tempers before the absolution had time to take. Now Killian knew the four cars by heart, knew what their owners would confess. Not one had committed a decent sin in years. The world has changed, he hankered to tell them; mortal sins have grown in stature.

He knelt for a minute in front of the altar hoping God would come out of hiding and make a difference. On the other hand there was the sanctuary lamp that had defied disbelief for centuries. What if the lamp was right and there was someone? Killian was not heroic. If there turned out to be an afterlife, he was nervous that it might, as promised, go on and on forever.

The big event in his priestly life had been the Second Vatican Council forty years earlier. Catholics went wild trying out new ideas. Many of them abandoned the confession box where once young girls told randy clerics their bad thoughts and men occasionally mumbled about having killed a neighbour.

Now only these four parishioners bothered to confess: a man, who always went first, and three women whose names were Mary, Patricia and Pauline. Pauline always went last. Killian often wondered why she used so much perfume just to go to confession. It was called Anais Anais, she had told him in a giddy moment. While the church had identified tons of sins over the centuries, some were neglected in practice, such as highway robbery and everyday swindling. Others, euphemistically referred to as the sixth and ninth, received most of the attention. Sex, in short. While most people were more embarrassed about sex than about highway robbery, Pauline had no such inhibitions. Killian went easy on the penance because God had created sex and no one wanted to offend God by belittling one of his brighter ideas.

When Margaret saw the priest's black Hyundai crawling up the lane, she warned the deceased Hughie to keep his mouth shut. Killian O'Loan had not visited the house for years, including the two years when Hughie was languishing and then dying. Now he surveyed the solid stone house with its dark red door and a turret to the side; a house with a pedigree. The ancestors were blue-blooded in some obscure way and their ghosts lived on. Killian squinted against the sun, taking the measure of the world. He had bushy white hair and a certain wildness. If he were a bigger man, and if he had a beard, he could pass for Moses, especially if he had ever climbed Mount Sinai.

'Margaret, are you there?'

'Why wouldn't I be?' The tone was stern. 'Amn't I always here?' She came forward with the strong handshake of a cattle dealer. She had a droll mouth and her face craggy thanks to the merciless weather. People said her hair had not been cut since before she married, and estimates ranged from several feet to half a mile of priceless tresses now turned white and wound tight on top of her head.

'I came to see the computer.' Killian had an aptitude for white lies. He had come to see Margaret, who, the neighbours said, was acting oddly and talking to Hughie at night.

'Ah that old thing,' she pointed at it with her finger at arm's length as if picking a criminal from a line-up. 'You'll drink a cup of tea anyway?'

'Why wouldn't I.' The house was perfectly tidy. A ginger cat slept in a wicker chair. The computer was hidden under plastic.

She clicked with the mouse once or twice and the whirring started. 'You'd wonder what's going on in there,' she said drily.

'Hughie is not in cyberspace,' Killian got down to business, 'and that's gospel.'

'Sure, don't I know.' She came out from the kitchen with a wooden tray and silver teapot and dark hard biscuits on a dish. 'Do you think, Father, is there anything after?'

'After?' Although he knew well what she meant.

'I'm beginning to think there isn't.'

They talked in a big circle while the ginger cat arched her back, hopped delicately to the floor and left.

Tuesday was golf with the lads, classmates since the seminary fifty-odd years earlier. Father Ignatius Swann, looking rakish and sleepy, was sitting on the clubhouse steps sucking a cigarette.

'Jaysus, Killian, isn't that a great day, what the fuck is keeping Louie?'

'He had a funeral or a sick call or some damn thing.'

'That fucker will kill himself working.' Iggy moved on to a fresh cigarette. He owned a very old set of clubs. When a parishioner gave him a state-of-the-art set he raffled it off to send a sick child to Lourdes. The parishioner huffed and took his business to another parish. 'Jesus wouldn't be caught dead with fancy golf clubs like that,' Iggy explained afterwards to the lads.

Louie arrived with apologies, a fat man sweating. They all

wore lookalike fawn slacks and bulky woollen sweaters in pastel colours, gifts from nieces and nephews. Yet it puzzled them when others identified them as priests a mile away.

'A three-ball, I suppose?' Killian said.

'Sure, what other option have we?'

A ghost came by. For half a lifetime there were four of them until Martin Evers died of lung cancer, the only one of them who had never smoked. They missed him at the golf where he was the weakest player but the best company.

'Do you think, lads, is there anything after?' Killian asked as they went around.

'Why wouldn't there?' Louie said.

'Jaysus, there'd better be,' Iggy was hacking in the long grass behind a tree. 'Otherwise we've endured all this fucking celibacy for nothing.'

'If there is something after,' Killian pressed on, 'and if Martin is there, wherever it is, would you not pray to him?'

'Pray for what?' Louie had little patience for introspection.

'Anything you want.'

'I wouldn't give the bastard the satisfaction of turning me down,' Iggy whacked the ball recklessly. He and the late Martin had fought tooth and claw over every shot of every game, but it was Iggy who had slept in a chair beside the sick bed for a fortnight until Martin said, 'Let me go.'

Killian had gone to confession to Martin for forty years. Wherever Martin had gone on to, he'd taken with him an intimate knowledge of Killian's soul, its ruts and drumlins. He would know, among other things, that Killian needed a new confessor. Louie had a theory that, one August day in 1965, as the Vatican Council sent spasms of reform across Christianity, priests stopped reading their divine office, Catholics stopped going to confession, and the clergy abandoned their belief in and then the practice of celibacy. All in one day, Louie said. A quantum leap, he called it. There were exceptions, Louie conceded. Killian was one of them: too cautious to risk going yonder without scraping the pot. But there was no chance he'd bare his soul's sores to Iggy or Louie. Sure, they could guess, and they'd be close to the mark. People, including the clergy, were strikingly similar. But, until you blurted out your sins you always had deniability; you might be an exception to the usual weaknesses and oddities.

'Do you think he sees us?' Louie asked. The world was full of novelty and news, but Martin kept demanding their attention. There was nothing like death to focus the mind. The golf used to be fiercely competitive, but now it didn't matter who won.

'The bastard had no right to go like that,' Iggy said.

'Come on out till I show you.'

'Who's this?'

'It's me. Margaret. Who did you think?' She was three sheets to the wind, cackling.

'This evening, so,' Killian O'Loan said.

Priests, the late Martin used to say, were cynical as judges. Still, they couldn't help thinking that some day a message might come. Nothing like the burning bush, those days were gone; it would probably be by phone, probably a parishioner with a conundrum, or nowadays the computer or some iPod thing. But nah, Killian thought, it wouldn't be Margaret, too close to home to be a messenger. He scratched himself and went to the grim green kitchen and made instant coffee. People will start talking. But anyone who knows me knows I'm not after her money. And as for sex: whatever about Margaret, they would never accuse me of bothering.

Margaret's computer was basking in the glow of a new brass lamp. Dusted and proud, yet patient and professional, computers had personalities if you gave them a chance; it wouldn't be long until they became household pets.

'Wait till I show you,' Margaret looked scrubbed and shining. Even the long hair—she must have washed it, which would be job enough, but drying it in this weather would be epic, unless she stuck her head in the clothes drier. She pulled up the new blue office chair. 'The letters keep moving around,' she complained. Killian stood behind her as the machine made the usual squeaky noises, distant and tentative, while it searched the world for whatever Margaret was about to reveal.

Most computer pictures don't make sense until you see the whole thing. This was even truer of Margaret's picture, which was from outer space.

'It's a nebula,' she said. 'The Elephant's Trunk Nebula.' It was the 'Astronomy Picture of the Day,' Killian read over her shoulder. A mighty ghost stalked across the screen. The figure, Margaret said, was composed of gas and dust and billions of stars. 'It's better than heaven, Father. A lot better than here.' Killian, like nearly everyone, had seen such pictures in popular magazines since the Hubble telescope was sent into orbit and began sending back cosmic wonders even astronomers had not dared to dream of.

'That's mighty, Margaret. Look at these fellows over here, crouching and running, like foxes through a thicket.' Killian pulled up the old wooden chair. 'Look at that yellow halo behind your fellow. And all the darkness beyond.'

'It's not yellow at all. It's photo filters they use. Aye. I was reading up on it there. Green for the hydrogen. Red for the sulphur. Blue for the oxygen. Oh aye.'

'God, Margaret, you know an awful lot.'

'I can read, can't I? That elephant's trunk is twenty light years long. Up in the universe, that's nothing. That nebula there is three thousand light years away. Do you know how far a light year is?'

'It's a lot.'

'It's six million million miles. Give or take a few kilometres. I looked it up.'

'And I suppose the little white dots are stars?'

'Stars, surely. Though some are whole systems. Galaxies, like. The rest is gas and dust. But interstellar dust isn't a bit like Irish dust. There's a new picture every day. I get up early to see them.'

Above the picture, it said: 2007 October 18.

'You're full of surprises, Margaret.' She was giddy. 'Who showed you?'

'You'll have the cup of tea anyway. I have cake.' She waddled off to the kitchen, protecting her sources. 'If only Hughie was here,' she said from the kitchen door. 'He loved the stars. He could point out Orion and the whole lot of them. But he knew nothing about that interstellar dust. Do you like porter cake, Father?'

'Why did you ask me out, Margaret?'

'Did I indeed?' She looked genuinely puzzled. 'It must be about the universe there. I thought you'd know more about it, where it all came from, but you seem as puzzled as myself.'

'I suppose you're referring to the Big Bang?' Once upon a time he would have told her childish yarns about the Garden of Eden, but that was ancient history.

'Aye, the Big Bang,' she said. 'The Big Bang is no bother, but then what happened?'

'You have me there.'

'Everything was sent flying. That's what it says.'

'That's powerful tea, Margaret.'

'Aye, my own blend. Look at this,' she changed the subject. It was said Hughie found her on a pilgrimage to the Reek. She was from Australia, neighbours explained, or was it Guam? Foreign anyway, they said. On the other hand she had the country brogue.

'That tea, Margaret. It's a pity to be wasting good whiskey on it.'

'Ah stop tormenting me.'

In June, Killian stacked turf in the little grate and put a match to it. Smoke swirled and he inhaled the nostalgia. He had no friends apart from the lads, who had no friends either, birds of a feather, wandering the earth in a post-Christian miasma and waiting for Christ to come back with a better public relations formula suitable for sceptical times.

He poured a healthy whiskey because he was nervous, then turned on the computer. The cosmos at my fingertips—Killian, like nearly everyone else, talked constantly to himself, though never out loud. He found the old envelope on which Margaret had scribbled the mysterious website: http://antwrp.gsfc.nasa/gov/apod/.

He picked October 5, 2007 at random: 'Starburst Cluster in NGC 3603.' The text said it was only 20,000 light years out in the Milky Way, our own backyard. Smack in the middle were thousands of incipient stars: piles of gas or rocks or red-hot fire like the sun, each up to two million years in the making, so the experts said. Not much happened in a day in outer space.

Northwest of the new cluster was a wisp of cloud. Billions upon billions of miles, Killian told himself, you'd get nowhere there in a light year. He was drawn into it, dodging intergalactic gas. He was sweating. *To be honest, I'm afraid. Who knows what awaits us. All that fire wasn't put there for nothing.* He ducked behind a toxic cloud, risked going a little further. In real life he always wanted to see what was over the hill. But up ahead was always more space, never what you were looking for.

In a panic he turned off the machine. Life used to be so simple back when the bishop told you what to think and there was nothing in the sky except the solid moon and wild geese flying past it in November.

On what seemed a normal Saturday the first three penitents came and went, leaving Killian alone with Pauline sifting through the debris of her life in search of sins. She admired kindness and constantly accused herself of meanness. She always left the sixth and ninth until last.

While she said her contrition, Killian peered stealthily through the slit in the red curtain to be sure the coast was clear. He gave her absolution with a vague wave of his hand. But he did not dismiss her as usual.

'I wonder would you do me a favour?'

'Well, sure,' she said in a hesitant stage whisper.

'Would you hear my confession?'

'What?'

'You heard—hear my confession.'

'You know I can't.'

'Yes, you can.'

'You're ordained and I'm not.'

'It's only a church law, Pauline. And around here I'm the church.'

'Are you feeling all right, Killian?' It was the first time she had ever called him by his name. 'This isn't a joke, by any chance?'

'I have no one else.'

'Sure, you do. I have to go now,' she sounded trapped, but gradually less determined. 'I wouldn't know where to begin.'

'First, you come in here, and I'll go round there.'

'Stay where you are, Father. William would kill me. Or you, more likely.' The reference was to her husband, a big, no-nonsense man.

'If I was to die tonight, how would you feel?'

'You'd better not tell me anything—well, anything serious.'

'Don't worry.' He opened the half-door. He looked away as he handed her the stole, and knew she was looking away too. He planted his arthritic knees on the wooden kneeler. He looked through the grill at Pauline, the stole around her neck in the gloom.

'How long?'

'That day is too good for golf,' Louie wiped the sweat from his neck with a pale blue handkerchief.

'How could it be too good?' Iggy threw a small tantrum. 'You need to lose weight, Louie, you fat hoor.'

The three bags of golf clubs sat upright in a huddle, like old crones bitching. All it took for the golfers to abandon their game was a large bird flopping down from the sky. The bird landed with a little run, not a clean landing like, say, a robin.

'It's a grouse,' Killian ventured.

'Grouse my arse,' Iggy countered, 'it's a pheasant.'

By the time they reached the clearing the bird had disappeared. So the talk turned to days of their youth. Louie hadn't seen a bird's nest since childhood. They searched among the bushes beside the fourth fairway. They found a thrush's well-made nest but nobody was home. They found a wren's mossy house complete with mossy roof and voted two to one against Iggy contaminating it by sticking his finger through the neat front door. They found several lost balls in the long grass. The golf course extended along a placid lake. Boats belonging to club members were tied to trees.

'Here's what we'll do,' Iggy said. 'We'll row over to the eighteenth hole and save ourselves a couple of hours.'

Killian juiced up the lawnmower, held his tongue between his teeth while he pulled the cord, then attacked the unruly grass. Down and up again. The mystic in him asked him why grass grew so well in July and not in January. Down and up and empty the box in the compost heap in the graveyard, there to rot before starting life over. Blackbirds flew in and out of the laurels keeping an eye on their territories.

God's house was as dumb and patient as a mountain. It never took sides in the battles over atheism or immorality. The round rose window looked unblinking across the countryside. It saw whins in the distance in fiery bloom. It saw fields of many colours when clouds filtered the sun. It saw tractors going mysterious places with hydraulic equipment, putting a shape on life. It saw, on the side of a hill, the heap of stones that was once a monastery. A lone gable with a gothic window presided over the ruins. The builders built the stone windows with special pride, not so much to honour God as to impress posterity—Killian knew a thing or two about ulterior motives.

I suppose this is destiny, he meditated. My vocation in life.

Including cutting the grass. If the bishop can't find a priest to replace me, a regular person will have to do. I offered more than twenty thousand Masses, way more, each a mighty undertaking if the theology is true. No wonder I'm tired. If Pauline can hear confessions, Patricia or someone can do the Mass. I'll coax them, bring them around. Or, as a last resort, a man. Men were never religious like women. We were too cocky to allow God to make a mess of things. The tide, though, is turning. If the women can be coaxed to save the world, I'll be happy to mow the grass and make little speeches when the footballers win a championship.

'Did you see November the first, Father?'

'Arp 87, is it?'

She sent him e-mails. 'Come on out,' she wrote, 'and I'll show you the Fairy of Eagle Nebula.' It was 'a stellar nursery,' she cackled when he got there. He wouldn't fall into space, not with Margaret there to grab him by the heels, figuratively at least, and hold him back. She said Arp was a bridge 75,000 light years long joining two swirling galaxies. 'Keep in mind, Father, there are billions of stars there, you need a substantial bridge. I have swiss roll to go with the tea, ye boy ye,' and she gave him a nudge with her elbow.

'Why don't we forget about the tea, Margaret, and drink the bloody whiskey the way God made it?'

The two galaxies, the experts said, were close enough to one another that their gravity caused them unearthly shuddering. 'But they're three hundred million light years from here,' Margaret said. 'We're safe as a house.'

'They look so harmless,' Killian agreed. 'Like two huge oysters away out there.'

'More like prawns,' she was in a contentious mood.

'Fishy anyway,' Killian said.

Came twilight on Saturday and the four cars outside Killian's church were joined by a fifth. It was a Mini Cooper, which, a generation or two earlier, was said by enthusiasts to be a flyer. Now, however, it was from a tired old relic that Father Iggy emerged. He kept his head low and glanced about furtively. He lit one further cigarette to focus his mind. He was wearing a gaberdine raincoat in spite of summer. He removed the outsize sunglasses, threw them on the passenger seat.

He splashed himself with holy water in the vestibule, then knelt at a safe distance. He had rehearsed for days and ran over his routine one last time as the whispering rose and fell in the confession box. If he could find anyone else, he rationalised, he wouldn't be going to Killian O'Loan. Yet one by one he eliminated all the other options, including the Redemptorists—too soft, he was told, not like the brawny days of old.

When the last penitent emerged, Iggy approached the box with a loud clatter, sending word ahead that a sinner of some consequence was in the neighbourhood. He pulled the curtain behind him. The little door slid aside in that familiar way. Iggy would not look directly but it was dark anyway. He must avoid flippancy and jocularity. One snide remark and Killian would boot him out.

'How long?'

Then Iggy realised there was something amiss. A pregnant pause followed. When he was asked a second time, it was definitely by a woman.

'What the fuck?' Iggy said.

'Watch your tongue, young man,'

'Who are you?'

'Are you here for confession?' Pauline asked.

'Where's Killian?'

'He's not here.'

'Jaysus, I know he's not here.'

'You must be a stranger,' Pauline grew conciliatory. 'We're giving Killian a break. So I'm doing the confessions. That man has been doing it for fifty years. Have you any idea?'

'No. No problem.' When a priest was young he learned the

ropes, made his mistakes and then settled down to a life of rote. Quick thinking was seldom needed. Iggy now made the snap decision to tough it out. This called for further snap decisions. He did his best. He told her it was thirty-five years. There were a few whoppers that he hadn't looked forward to telling Killian, but he had no trouble telling a stranger. Fuck her. He saw no reason to inform her of his clerical status. The devil might be in the details where status was concerned. Afterwards there was silence. He couldn't help noticing the pungent Anais Anais. The odour of sanctity—he was shaken by his ordeal and dying for a joke.

'Anything else?'

'No, that's it.'

'I don't wish to burst your bubble,' she then said, 'but there's nothing here worth absolving.' Silence from Iggy. 'Have you forgotten what mortal sin is?' She didn't wait for an answer. 'Eternal damnation and all that. Gehenna, you know? Confession is not a cure-all for people's insecurities and broken dreams, young man.'

'I'm not a young man.' It was no joke. He could never even tell Killian—the seal was in play. 'Why don't you give me absolution anyway,' he pleaded, 'and I won't bother you again.'

The year pushed the months aside. Winter brought long nights for taking stock. Above the sky, beyond the sunshine and the drizzle, Killian told the lads playing a brisk round of golf in November, there was unbelievable life struggling to succeed. The universe was a pup. Out near the edges, where it hurtled through clean, fresh space, rubble from the Big Bang was still taking shape and turning green with the help of occasional showers, and sunshine from immense suns was making scenery to match Killarney and the Mourne Mountains.

When he saw Louie and Iggy exchanging glances, he gave up.

'Take a gander at this,' Margaret was at the computer when he arrived.

'Stand up,' Killian ordered, and when she did he hugged her.

'Life is a funny old entity, Margaret. I don't understand a bit of it.'

'Goodness,' she said.

'I know. It won't happen again.' Yet he thought her almost handsome, a stately widow, and wondered how long it had been since the late Hughie and herself had their final kerfuffle. Neither of them would have known it was the last time, that was life. Margaret was dressing more nattily lately: moss-green dresses with elaborate stitching down to her Reebok runners.

'It looks like a map of the USA,' he said over her shoulder. 'New York here and Seattle over there.' The picture was dated October 7th, 2007.

'It is a map,' Margaret confirmed. He thought of her looking for stars in the skies of Guam in her childhood, and she with honey-coloured braids already several feet long. 'There are two million galaxies in that map,' she said. 'Each with hundreds of billions of stars. Put that in your pipe and smoke it.'

'There must be an odd moon, so.' Killian and Margaret sat side by side in front of the computer, although the computer was practically invisible and all they saw was cyberspace—the cosmos and its wonders.

'Aye, moons, too.' The cat slept on. Logs burned in the spacious fireplace and smoke scampered up the chimney and off into the ether. Eventually she sauntered off to make the tea. If she had gone to astronomy school in Guam, instead of whatever she did, she would be a legend now, with a telescope named after her just like Hubble.

'Look at this one,' she said after the tea, and conjured up January 6th, 2006 from the archives—the Tarantula Nebula, a region of spectacular colour. 'It's a star forming region,' she explained, 'a thousand light years across.'

'It's mighty,' Killian said.

'Are you blind, you silly man?' It was a harsh night outside. Gales blew in from the ocean and stripped the last leaves from shuddering trees. Margaret's house whimpered. It was the kind of night you thought you heard music until you decided it was only the wind. 'Follow me down here,' she spoke with the authority of the blue-blooded, all piss and vinegar, and traced her old finger along the Tarantula Nebula, coming to rest on a green glob tinged with yellow. 'There's dry land there. Can you not see it?'

'I believe I do,' Killian said without conviction.

'Surrounded by shining seas? And mountains easing themselves down to green lakes. And by the lakes, cattle—you must see them?'

'I do indeed.'

'Not just cattle. Deer and sheep. And is that not a lion lying down with the lamb?'

'It is, it is.'

'But that's nothing. See the firmament, with separate suns for morning, noon and night. And moons floating to keep the tides on time. Birds and bees, including cuckoos dancing jigs in meadows. And corncrakes—the poor corncrake safe at last from mowers and the fumes of diesel.'

'Go on,' he encouraged.

'Look at the trees. I'd swear that's a weeping willow. And yonder, a holly bush with berries. Over there—isn't that a city? But no car crashes, or cars either, or dog shite in the streets, no guns or brigadier generals or graveyards or even hairdressers or TV commercials. And you know why? Because they're getting on famously without them.'

'But the people?'

'They're so advanced you can't see them. Is there anything left in that bottle?'

They drank the whiskey from two blue mugs. 'I hope Hughie won't be vexed,' Margaret said. 'He had great respect for whiskey.' Other family members were upstairs in bed, Killian knew, all ghosts. May they rest in peace, he prayed.

'The people are spiritual,' Margaret could see cyberspace more clearly after the whiskey. 'Did you notice their houses have no doors? That's because they're—what's the word for it?—

ubiquitous, I suppose. In and out, whoosh, and Bob's your uncle.'

'Look at them rusty buckets.'

Margaret didn't want to know. The secret was to dodge black holes and supernovas, skirt the ultraviolet radiation and intergalactic dust. Out at the outer edges, life was fresh. There was more scope and incentive for planets to grow grass and produce frogs and linnets and plovers and even dinosaurs, and for people to become sheer as the wind and after that build whatever they would build.

'Do you hear the music?' Killian said.

'Aye, surely, I hear it,' Margaret agreed. 'It's the galaxies banging into each other and sorting out huge issues.'

The trick, Killian was sure, was to sidestep the rowdy regions, be alert for the serene spaces, for the little surprises, for temperate climates and good neighbours and an odd dandelion to make you feel at home.

The Friendship Portfolio

My name is Olaf, a quiet man to whom not much happens. Yet every life stumbles, sooner or later, on some unusual occurrence worth writing down. Mine found me in a Chicago suburb some years ago, driving a rented car amid all the four-way stops. Ahead of schedule, I drove more slowly. One doesn't want to be late for a suicide, but one doesn't want to be indecently early either.

I parked on the street. In such a neighbourhood, I figured, the red car will be stolen by midnight, but it's not mine. It wasn't a slum but a motley, colour-blind area where idealists lived side by side with the underprivileged. Colette was an idealist. The white frame house needed paint. She was the sort who wouldn't paint hers if her neighbours couldn't afford the same. As a matter of fact she wouldn't paint it anyway. There were no curtains in the windows, also typically Colette. Normally I fail to notice such things, but one pays closer attention to those about to die. Doomed as we all are to mortality, it makes sense to be morbid. There were a few daffodils inside the broken gate, though they could be tulips, I'm no good at flowers.

She came out to greet me. My imagination had been doing somersaults since this odd episode got off the ground. Would she be sad or glad or spooky or what? Would she be emaciated and a mess? Ought I to be solemn or my morosely jocular self? Colette just grinned, surprisingly serene.

'I was getting worried,' she said. As if I were the one to be worried about. She was fifty-five, I had figured it out. And not a bit emaciated. Fifteen years since I saw her, give or take. She was wearing jeans and a faded pink shirt. This must be the style, then, for such occasions.

'I hope I'm not late.' I thought it was a neat little joke to break the ice, but she didn't seem to get it.

We were never more than good friends. At Loyola she aimed to be a therapist of some sort, while I aimed to be, I'm embarrassed to admit, a screenwriter. Over sloppy sandwiches in cheap restaurants I discovered Colette had a more lively imagination than my own, and could conjure up stories Hollywood would kill for—she said so herself. Even when a story ran out of steam she had humour galore to get it through the bad times. I, meanwhile, couldn't help believing I'd make a better therapist than Colette. Whatever therapy was—what I had in mind was short cuts to befriending the insane, which was nearly everyone.

We went our ways. We married other people, marriages that did not take. I landed in San Francisco, without encumbrances, editing the half-baked books of people eager to leave posterity a message. Colette stuck doggedly to the therapy thing. Once she found she could make only a miniscule difference in people's lives, she placed herself at the disposal of the very rich, who, she insisted, had a right to be indulged as well. It was around this time we drifted apart. There were children, but I couldn't remember the details. Except for one thing: in the throes of her sour divorce she asked me, in the event of her demise, to be executor of her will. In short, to look after the children. Such a likelihood seemed remote at the time, and it would have been churlish to refuse. Then I forgot about it.

Until a day when the phone startled me—Colette. She had stumbled on my name, she said, and tracked me down. It was a lie. After several nostalgic conversations she came to the point: she was dying. Galloping cancer, she called it, though I presumed this was not a technical term. She would need my signature, she reminded me pointedly, on account of my being her executor.

'How soon?' The past was not an abstraction. It was full of people clawing at the present. For a moment I resented her wily manoeuvre. Yet we're all strangely civilised considering the age we live in. Good feelings floated back, collected from irrecoverable yesterdays. Because memories couldn't be bought or sold, they were priceless. Love didn't enter into it, but perhaps it was friendship, a taken-for-granted idea that still roamed the world working wonders.

It was a matter of weeks, Colette said.

'What about chemo and all that?'

'No use,' she said. 'Once cancer starts galloping even chemo can't slow it.' I never bothered to check the veracity of this. She let the cat out of the bag a little at a time. She planned to manage her departure, leaving nothing to chance.

'You mean suicide?' the penny dropped.

'Who mentioned suicide?'

'Then you don't know when.'

'I'll know.' There followed a pregnant pause. 'I'll let you know.'

After that, the nearly daily calls went silent for a month. I began to think she might have drifted back out of my life as unceremoniously as she had reentered it. This was a relief: I was having enough trouble steering my own small destiny. Yet it was also a relief when she phoned again. She had not discarded me. One wants to matter. The search for meaning eventually takes every searcher down peculiar byways. There was also, I confess, the curiosity factor. I wanted to know what she'd do and how she'd do it, what she'd say, who would be there. It was death, after all—life at its most intense in a paradoxical way. When death is in the neighbourhood you want to look the other way, but first you want to steal a glance.

The event—or, as she still insisted, the non-event—would be the following Thursday. Around six. It sounded at the same time precise and casual, like cocktails or a barbecue. She sounded very alive, even upbeat, why would anyone want to walk away from such seeming contentment? It crossed my mind that this might be a perverse practical joke or, worse, some kind of scam. She gave me directions. As I jotted them down I wondered where all this information would go after Thursday. All the things she had learned, the memories and jokes and even her knowledge of myself: could they go out of existence so readily, give themselves up? The jury was still out on the afterlife.

Now she stood between the door and me. From a breast pocket she withdrew a packet of Marlboro and a battered book of matches. There was no further need to worry about the killing power of cigarettes. For the rest of this waning day the smallest incidentals would become larger than life. Bluntly stated, Colette would not come through this door tomorrow. Old age was for getting used to going, for wearing oneself out so that the end would seem a good idea. But Colette was fifty-five and blithe. That was the treachery of cancer, especially the galloping kind. Her hair was as grey as my own. I would not have recognised her. And vice versa, I concluded dolefully. One did not need cancer to look like us.

'Who's inside?'

'The kids,' she said.

'If they can't stop you, I guess neither can I?'

'Stop me from what?'

'I don't know. What are you going to do?'

'You may have a story you can sell at last.'

'I'd prefer it to be fiction.'

'Vinnie's not here.' Vinnie was twenty-six, the youngest.

'Is there a reason?'

'There's always a reason. I wish I knew what.' She led the way inside. I wasn't sad. I didn't love her. I didn't pity her. I liked her, I surely must have, to come two thousand miles. Friendship drew us back together. Although I didn't know what friendship was. It was bloodless, devoid of passion, almost boring, yet people go to great lengths for it.

Inside, the house was surprisingly spacious.

'You remember Noelle,' though she surely knew I didn't. Noelle came forward with a generous hug. She would be thirty-one now—I had figured out all their ages. 'And Louis,' Colette added. He would be thirty. More formal, not ready to be friendly. 'And my friend Freda, who is a nurse. And an expert on everything,' Colette added with a touch of sarcasm.

'Expert enough to know this is crazy,' Freda got down to business. Her accent was slightly foreign; I concluded for no good reason that she came from Eastern Europe. She was a large, energetic woman.

'I agree,' Noelle said. I had landed in the middle of a debate. Freda came striding with a tray of sandwiches. Louis followed with coffee. There was no word of booze, on an evening when booze would have done the local population a world of good. I was, I realised, quite hungry, but it seemed inappropriate to get over-involved with food at such a time. Gradually we settled, sat around, little plates precarious on our knees, eating as much as seemed decent. That included Colette, who took three pieces of cake. A stately grandfather clock with a tarnished pendulum indicated it was almost seven. The television was on though the sound was inaudible—there seemed to have been an explosion in some foreign country, a close-up of silent blood on a wet street.

'What's crazy?' I asked Freda, who seemed most likely to give me the straight dope.

'What she's doing,' Freda nodded in the direction of Colette laboriously climbing the stairs to the bathroom.

'And what's that?'

'She's in pain,' Noelle chirped. Too chirpy, I thought. She was very attractive behind the long blonde hair, one strand carefully draped over her left eye. 'She has decided to terminate the pain. But surely she must have told you that,' she challenged me, 'or you wouldn't be here?'

'It's called suicide,' Louis said. He had one eye on the mute television.

'No, it's not,' Noelle fired back.

Colette, wan and grave, stood undecided in the doorway. Louis slid sideways to make room on the black leather sofa. She sat and kissed him on the cheek, but he turned his face away.

'I wonder what's keeping Tom,' she frowned at her watch. No one ventured an opinion on this.

Freda was collecting abandoned coffee cups with fierce determination. I had decided she came from Estonia, from farming stock, my adrift mind idling.

'Who's Tom?' I asked.

'An old friend,' Colette said.

'Boyfriend,' Noelle corrected. 'He won't be here.'

'Yes, he will,' Colette said without conviction, glancing at the old clock.

'He's not a gallant man,' Noelle said to me.

'I'll grant you, he doesn't approve,' Colette conceded.

'Doesn't care,' Noelle said.

'Stop it,' Louis shouted in a controlled way, 'for God's sake, stop it.' He was assistant manager at a nearby Wall-Mart store. He was wearing a red track suit and white joggers. Got them on special, the unkind thought passed through my mind. He seemed to be in great psychic pain. Years ago, I had carelessly made a pledge to cherish him and Noelle and the absent Vinnie if anything should happen to Colette.

The perky sound of a cell phone came from the next room. Colette jumped up to answer. Freda took her place on the sofa. She wore a loose, navy blue garment that was probably a nurse's outfit. She folded her muscular arms, sighed.

'It's what she wants to do,' Freda said. 'It's not suicide. It's enough medication to kill the pain. There is no rule about how much is correct. It's just, you know, she does not want to be, I don't know, like this,' Freda spread her hands to indicate the whole world in its current sorry state.

'She'll die, Freda,' Louis said. 'Isn't that why we're here?'

Colette's raised voice came through from the next room.

'No one has all the answers,' Freda said. 'No one has a word for this.' Her hair was chopped short. She had given up on beauty years ago, and settled on efficiency as a substitute. 'So you have no right to call it suicide.'

Dusk was settling over Chicago. Through the window I could see brisk white birds flying by beyond apple trees. Not symbolism, I admonished myself, they were just doves or doves' cousins. Colette had managed to assemble only a poor collection of friends in fifty-five years. Especially me. I had no solutions, no jokes, no song to sing, no money to ease whatever money eased. And it seemed, furthermore, I was in good company, unable between us to ease even one soul from Chicago to wherever Colette hoped to go.

'At eight,' Freda said. 'She takes her medication at eight sharp.'

'He says he's busy,' Colette interrupted from the doorway. 'Can you believe it?'

'You don't need him, Mom,' Noelle said.

'How do you know?' The joy had gone out of Colette. She looked frail enough to die without outside intervention. She flecked a long cylinder of cigarette ashes on the carpet. Louis handed her an ash tray. She banged it down on a table. 'Someone vacuum the carpet tomorrow, OK?' Louis led her to a big ugly chair. 'I wanted you all here,' Colette said, while the old clock measured the night. 'I wanted Vinnie here.'

'And Vinnie wanted his inheritance,' Louis said. 'Everything goes to Noelle's kids,' Louis rather pointlessly explained to me.

'Poor Olaf,' Colette said, confirming my own view that she had forgotten about me. 'I hope you understand.'

'Not much,' I said.

'I should have married you, Olaf.'

'We had good times, Colette. Marriage would have spoiled them.'

'That's what I mean. I should have fallen in love with you. Then these two would be ours,' she gestured toward Louis but not Noelle. 'I wish I knew how to do this gracefully.'

'We could try a singalong,' Louis said with what I took to be sincerity.

'Amazing grace,' Freda sang quietly, yet loud enough to silence the room. 'How sweet the sound,' her big voice grew louder, a force of nature. 'I once was lost but now I'm found, was blind but now I see.' Noelle was first to join in. I added my own timid contribution, never melodious. Then Louis came in, surprisingly robustly, until the beautiful hymn filled the house. Colette did not sing, she sobbed instead. Then Noelle cried a little, and Louis looked shaken but sang doggedly on. Freda remained grey and solid like a rock. No matter what happens, I decided at that point, I'll be on the afternoon flight tomorrow.

The clock pointed to 7:40.

'Try Vinnie one more time,' Colette said to Noelle.

'I don't know why you bother,' Noelle said. 'He's the favourite,' she explained to the room as she left.

'There are no favourites,' Colette said. 'Right now, I love everyone.' I observed her every twitch and expression, every cigarette, waited for each segment of ashes to fall on the carpet. There was no sign her resolve would falter. 'At eight I'll take my medicine,' she said to everyone. 'It's only medication. To kill the pain, you know?' She went to the bathroom again. Freda went to the kitchen, took the phone off the hook, then went to the front room and turned off the cell phone. I was practically invisible among them, shadowing everyone, seeing everything. I saw Colette watch Freda as she disconnected the phones. I saw her shrug. Impossible to see what was in her mind. I had never thought her organised enough to pull off a turn like this.

'I was thinking, Olaf, of that dog you used to have,' she said as she held out her arms for a hug. 'The black dog. I always hated that animal.'

'I'm sure sorry about that, Colette.'

'I wish we had kept in touch. Who knows how things would have gone.' It was a desperate embrace, the desperation more mine than hers. There must be something to say, some more agreeable way to cross over. I didn't tell her I never had a dog.

Next she hugged Louis. Neither of them spoke.

'Tell Vinnie I'm sorry,' she said as she hugged Noelle.

'I'll tell him. Vinnie would be here if he could.'

'I know he would. Tell the babies I love them, that they were on my mind.'

'They'll miss you.'

'And I'll miss them.'

'Are you sure about this, Mom? You could put it off until later.' The rest of us stood in a row as the clock chimed eight.

'Of course I'm not sure,' Colette said. 'But there are so few alternatives.'

'We could go out to dinner, you'd enjoy that. Or we could order in pizza and I'd go get the kids and we'd have a party.'

'If you see Tom, tell him I'm sorry I yelled at him.'

'I'll tell him.'

'Thanks for everything, Freda,' and she hugged the big woman.

'Everything will be fine,' Freda said.

'Let's go, then,' and she led the way into the dining room, which had a bed with two white pillows. It looked like an infirmary. There were roses in a vase on the window sill. There were plastic chairs by the wall, just like a waiting room, but I was the only one to sit, a witness, I told myself, on behalf of those who were not there but cared nonetheless.

'You're sure this is painless?' Louis had eleventh-hour qualms.

'It will be very peaceful,' Colette gave him another hug and pushed him into a chair.

'If there is any, you know, distress, or whatever, I'm leaving.'

'You were always thoughtful, baby.' She sat on the side of the bed. 'It's not how I would have wanted it, either.' She looked at us as if she might try to explain. She was rich now, she had told me. Her therapy books had been translated everywhere. The sporty Mercedes in the driveway was presumably hers. I never imagined she would become wealthy, never thought she would get galloping cancer. 'I don't know what other way to do it,' was all she said. She had no speech prepared.

'Time for your medication,' Freda said.

'Good old Freda. I love you.'

She stretched herself on the bed. Freda produced a faded quilt and draped it over her, tucked it under her chin.

'My grandmother's,' Colette explained, glancing sideways.

The ritual itself was bleakly banal. A few pills on a saucer: one moment they were there, inert and harmless, then they were out of sight, doing their work. Freda held the glass of water poised, her strong other arm behind Colette's head, urging the water on her until the glass was half-empty, then gone. Why could Colette not go wild and crazy and fill us all, including herself, with drink, before going out in a paroxysm of good cheer? Death just refused to be taken lightly.

'We could say a prayer, mother?' Noelle suggested in a tentative way. We had crossed the line beyond which the usual procedures did not apply.

'Sing that song again,' Colette said, looking straight at the plaster ceiling.

'Amazing grace,' Noelle sang, and the others picked it up. Freda hovered at the foot of the bed, her wide face inscrutable. The haunting words filled the room and went out the door and away. I could not sing. Something might happen, some breakthrough. The medical world seldom sang over its pills. Colette closed her eyes. She might be falling asleep or dying or just thinking, maybe seeing her life flash by as some say it does. She withdrew her hand from under the quilt, extended it. Noelle held the hand. Colette glanced at us a few times. Some last word would be priceless, any old word. There had been so little explanation, so little context. When the hymn came to an end, the singers started over, but the energy had gone out of it.

Outside the window, darkness descended. Louis quietly left the room. He's just going to the bathroom, I decided; I need to go myself.

When Colette's eyes remained closed for several minutes, it seemed she had departed. So quietly, with so little drama, it was a letdown.

Then, as if to prove me wrong, there was the flicker of an eyelid and she opened her eyes. She looked around. She looked startled. She became pensive, and frowned, as if seeking her bearings. She then threw back the quilt, threw her legs over the side of the bed, stood up, a little uncertainly. Freda grabbed her by the arm. She pulled away.

'Where are my cigarettes?' she asked, irritated.

'You need to get back into bed,' Freda ordered.

Louis came in from the front room with the cigarettes and battered matches. Colette took them eagerly, lit one.

This part of the story no one will believe. One could never put it in a screenplay.

'How do you feel, Mom?' Noelle asked.

'How do you think I feel?'

'The medicine was just right,' Freda said, a little defensively. 'It will work soon.'

'It's not too late to get you to the emergency room,' I ventured. From here on, it wouldn't be suicide. It would be death by misadventure or some other vague mishap.

'Why would I do that?' Colette snapped. Something had happened while she was—I don't know—away, I suppose. She wasn't, in short, as friendly. All the plots she once had for the movies—where were they now? I stood aside as she walked unsteadily to the living room.

'We love you, mother,' Louis said, walking behind her. 'We just don't know what to do.'

'Where's Tom?' Colette asked.

'Tom couldn't make it,' Louis said.

'Is there an ash tray?'

I grabbed one and Noelle grabbed another. Colette smiled for the first time since returning from wherever she had been. At this point she confronted me.

'I always loved you, Olaf,' she said. 'I couldn't go without telling you.'

'Is that why you came back?'

'Even if it's not true, say you loved me too.'

'I loved you too, Colette,' I lied.

She seemed relieved. She turned back to the others. Sat in the ugly chair.

'Did you feel anything, Mom?' Noelle asked.

'Feel what?'

'I don't know. When you were, I guess, asleep, what was it like?'

'I was sleepy, that was all it was.' She lit another cigarette. 'Say hi to the babies,' she said to Noelle, 'and tell them I love them.'

'You're tired,' Freda said soothingly. 'Lie down on the sofa.'

'This is ridiculous,' Colette said. She didn't know with whom to be angry. If only she could grab some amazing grace and get happy. And forget the craven Tom. Spend one slow cigarette of quality time in the bosom of her family, then off to eternity.

'Thanks, Olaf,' she seemed to notice me at irregular intervals. If she would go now, I would be one of her famous last words. 'Put me down,' she said, and flopped on the sofa. Stoic Freda put a cushion under her head and the quilt over her. She shuddered, and clouds crossed her face, and the eyes closed. She seemed to suffer no pain. The medication, in other words, worked.

There is a whole folklore about people not being dead, about coming back from practically beyond and telling secrets from the other side. Colette knew now, could tell all: a script Hollywood would kill for.

In about an hour, Freda said she was definitely dead. From cancer, she added.

We went together to Perkins for dinner.

'Did you know her well, Olaf?' Louis asked.

'Years ago. We were good friends.'

The Film Society

Robin Williams is John Keating, the new teacher in an elite boys' school. He exhorts the lads to vie with life before they grow old and die. *Carpe diem* sums up his attitude. This could legitimately be regarded as either horse sense or poppycock, but to people of a certain age it is sheer nostalgia for what might have been.

'Time out,' Bernadette O'Hara says, and her husband Victor presses the remote. Time out is shorthand for a trip to the toilet. That was quick, Victor thinks. Old bladders are a punishment, like death itself, for original sin or something. When Bernadette was young her bladder had great staying power, I can hardly remember her having to go. Victor's head is a cauldron of introspection, though no one suspects this. He is a thin, pale man with thin, straight lips likely to confound the best lip reader. His eyes fondly follow Bernadette to the bathroom: Bernadette with girth enough for two, and a beautiful face surrounded by flaming, curly hair; a jolly, arthritic, out-of-breath girl of seventy-five.

'It always makes me sad,' Lili sighs at Victor's elbow.

'No need to be lugubrious, Lili,' Dr Freele says silkily, 'it's only a film.'

'I don't know about lugubrious,' Lili responds frostily. 'I feel sad, that's all.' Lili is a diminutive, pretty person who boldly wears her white hair down to her backside. If she dyed it, Victor speculates, I'd woo her. Bernadette would never notice. Around here nobody notices the obvious.

'You're only sad, Lili, because you didn't *carpe diem*,' Dr Freele purrs. 'Like myself, I suppose, and I, at least, had my chances.'

The acid words float in space as Bernadette shuffles back to her sturdy chair. The room is full of thoughts. Lili searches her head for a lethal response to Dr Freele's jibe. Dr Freele loathes herself for the mean-spirited woman she has become. She is eighty-two now. It is forty years since she saw a classroom but she insists on being called doctor. She once wrote a scholarly book about culture that was lauded on three continents, until it went out of print, and she hopes vaguely to be rediscovered soon. Though a self-described intellectual she considers style a sine qua non and devotes most of her nest egg to jewellery.

'Off you go, Victor,' Bernadette says. Robin Williams is urging anarchy on the lads. *Carpe diem* also means kick the other fellow's arse.

One student wants to be an actor but his constipated father wants him to be a clone of his constipated self. The father is at a disadvantage, Victor knows, because of the son's trump card: youth. The impatient son, however, commits the ultimate impatience: suicide. Victor knows all this in advance. He has sat through this film hundreds of times. It's too late to hope for a happy ending. Victor and Bernadette and Lili and Dr Freele know a thing or two about the cinema; they know better than to think out loud.

Another student is fighting a losing battle with his libido. Lili, each time life gives love a try, cheers it on, go on, go on. But when Lothario goes on he gets a bloody nose.

'Time out,' Bernadette announces again. A tray has been prepared in the kitchen. Several tea bags are waiting in the teapot. There is a plate with fruit cake and another with digestive biscuits. Bernadette can tell you who will eat what, this ritual being regular as the seasons.

They were all young when the cinema was young. They

practically grew up with Mary Pickford, Charlie Chaplin, Joan Crawford, John Barrymore. They watched *Mutiny on the Bounty*, *Double Indemnity*, *The Grapes of Wrath* and other films that became milestones of human progress just when the human race needed a new shake-up. One thing led to another: film led to television, videos, DVDs and other novelties.

More than twenty years ago, a group of friends formed the Film Society. They would rent down-at-heel cinemas during off-hours, or borrow a room at the local school when 16mm became an option. The Film Society became a legend just in time to start going downhill. One had only to mention it and people would grow nostalgic about film noir, the westerns, the new wave, neorealism, the musicals.

Even when video made it possible to take the cinema home, a band of diehards clung to the Film Society. I'd say we're here for the company, except that we don't enjoy the company, Victor sometimes ponders. There were once hundreds, then dozens. They met in each others' homes. They would bake apple pies or make trifle to spice up the intermission, which was *de rigueur*. Then life got a few years older and people found excuses not to bother. So Bernadette said she and Victor would play host. Soon there were only the four of them, and no more apple tart. We all have our reasons, Victor meditates. Mine, I think, is I love Lili. Of course I still love Bernadette but love is elastic and can easily be stretched to include Lili.

Robin Williams gets the sack near the end. It's only fiction, Lili thinks, but still. When the students seize the day and stage a demonstration, some equilibrium is restored to life. Victor rewinds the video. As the years passed, their interest was sustained by an ever-dwindling number of pictures, what they called the classics.

'I've been meaning to mention it,' Dr Freele disturbs the tranquility of the evening. 'I have a friend who would like to join.' She is bundling herself up for the short walk home, grey coat over grey sweater, all tweedy and just right for the jewellery.

'Oh,' Bernadette says.

'I thought I should mention it. His name is Henry. I was hoping next Wednesday would be suitable.'

'Well, certainly,' Victor says, fussing with the remote. Everyone is fussing with something.

'Certainly,' Lili echoes Victor. 'It must be ten years since we had a guest.'

'He doesn't want to be a guest. He'd like to be a member.'

'That would go further back. That would be yourself, Dr Freele.'

'If you all agree that it's not appropriate, I can disinvite him.'

'Oh, not at all,' Bernadette says. 'That is, if he's already invited. What do you think, Lili?'

'Oh, sure,' Lili says vaguely, and the diplomatic dance winds down.

'Goodbye, goodbye,' Victor says to Dr Freele, then to Lili, 'goodbye, goodbye.' Once they are out the door he moves stealthily back to the television where Barcelona is playing Inter Milan in the UEFA Cup.

'What do you make of that?' Bernadette asks when they reach half-time in Barcelona.

'It's a bit odd.'

On Wednesdays Bernadette badgers Victor to do a little vacuuming, a little dusting, and arrange everybody's chair in its proper place. This Wednesday she badgers more so because of the guest. Victor checks the machine to be sure the movie is ready for lift-off. As the years passed even the classics lost their lustre until one November night they all agreed they felt most content watching *Dead Poets Society*.

Dr Freele and the guest arrive together in his little white Citroën. Lili peers between the curtains of the O'Hara parlour.

'He's in the right age bracket, anyway,' she says with a hint of satisfaction.'

'This is Henry,' Dr Freele proceeds with the introductions.

'I'm here because I promised,' he says as if he were doing the others a favour. He is a large red-faced man, full of energy. He has a droopy moustache, and little trendy spectacles too small for his face. His demeanour is blustery, he could never enter a room without a stir. 'Thank you for having me,' he says, and the others make noises to suggest their pleasure.

On a typical Wednesday, after a brief flurry of small talk and a last trip to the loo, they would get straight to the film. But Henry is already draped across Victor's recliner and telling his new friends the highlights of his life. A former shoe salesman, his real love was the amateur stage. He has played everything from John B. Keane to Shakespeare. Prodded along by Dr Freele, he throws out references to Pirandello, Ibsen, John Gielgud.

If he shuts up long enough, Victor thinks, I'll tell him about the time I ran the London marathon. Even Bernadette doesn't believe me. Flamboyant is the word, Lili is thinking, a little less flamboyant would suit the Film Society.

'My big moment almost came,' Henry is saying, 'when I got a small role in a London production of 'Peer Gynt.' But I caught a dose of the flu, and I was a has-been before I even got started.' Now they see the face of a humbled man. It would be different if he had done that 'Peer Gynt' thing, and perhaps gone on from there to Broadway, Victor thinks, he would now be a more boisterous humbug.

'During those halcyon days I dreamed, as every actor does, of making it to Hollywood.'

'There's still time,' Dr Freele encourages.

'Thank you,' Henry beams at her. Every word is a performance. 'I am not one ever to say never, but I'm looking eighty in the eye and it's time I settled down.' The self-mockery helps as they sway between liking and detesting him. 'On the other hand, I wouldn't be the first to stumble into Hollywood by accident and land on my feet in that topsy-turvy madhouse.'

'Would anyone like a drink?' Victor asks in the hush that follows Henry's speech. Bernadette will think I've gone mad, he thinks, out of my mind. We're forty-five minutes behind schedule, but

I don't hate him the way I thought I would. So Henry accepts a beer and the girls glasses of white wine.

'*Un Chien Andalou* is, in my opinion, the culmination of the silent cinema,' Henry is still expounding, 'though some say that distinction should go to Carl Dreyer's *Passion of Joan of Arc*. If you wished to show them, I happen to know where you can rent them in the city.'

Fat chance, Lili sips the wine. What he forgets is all the thoughts we have, between us, piled up over the years. There's very little that hasn't occurred to us already. But still, we seem to be having fun.

'And then there's Hollywood. Who will ever forget Buster Keaton and W. C. Fields and the Marx Brothers? As luck would have it, I ran into Groucho in a restaurant not long ago.'

'Really?' Bernadette says. 'I thought he'd died years back.'

'I wouldn't swear what year it was,' unflappable Henry raises his glass in a salute to good times, 'but it was definitely before he died.' He downs the beer with the enthusiasm of a famished sailor, holds up the empty glass. 'I never drink more than two beers, but I never drink less.' He laughs a big guffaw. He does that guffaw well, Dr Freele thinks. He's definitely jolly, Lili is glad people are not all cut from the same cloth.

'We might as well make a night of it,' Victor returns with the beer. Bernadette pours more wine. Lili is feeling tipsy but is happy to meet the bottle halfway.

'But what I like best,' Henry has a few more bons mots up his sleeve, 'is the Europeans. From Murnau and G. W. Pabst on to the incomparable Jean Renoir, the Europeans were, between ourselves, more sophisticated. Sure, there have been lean periods, but think of Eisenstein, and the French *Nouvelle Vague*, and the Italians, *The Bicycle Thief* and all.'

He has stored up a ton of information in his head, Victor is thinking, for an occasion like this, and now we're it. The hen can't wait to lay the egg.

'Do you like Woody Allen?' Lili asks.

'A lightweight. Overrated all the way from here to Hollywood. Nothing he wouldn't do for a cheap laugh.'

'I had tea with him once.' She tries to distance herself from the fast-fading comedian. 'It was in New York, years ago. My cousin worked for his wife once a week, cleaning and that. I don't even remember which wife it was.'

'I know the feeling,' Henry generously opts to lay bare his own vulnerability. 'Back when John Huston lived in that castle in Galway, I would rent a cabin down the road in hopes of running into him. But there wasn't a single sighting.' There is a brief pause to lament what might have been. 'Serves him right,' and Henry does another guffaw.

'I never liked John Huston,' Lili says, getting back at the maestro for belittling Woody Allen.

'I often ask myself,' Henry goes on, 'what I would say if someone asked what was my favourite film. But since no one's asked me, I'm going to tell you anyway.' There are two bottles of Stella Artois left on the coffee table, and Henry, without interrupting his sentence, slips one over beside his glass. 'Bergman's *The Seventh Seal* will always be my favourite. How can it get better than life and death playing chess for the upper hand? It was an act of God that Max Von Sydow and Ingmar Bergman should be on earth at the same time.'

The Seventh Seal my arse, Victor silently fulminates, while Bernadette glances at her watch causing a chain reaction.

'Just look what time it is,' Lili says.

'Victor has everything ready,' Bernadette says as Victor fondles the remote.

'Forgive me,' Dr Freele intervenes, 'I should have mentioned it before, but we were having such a good time.' She is flustered and apologetic. 'What I mean is, Henry brought a film we might like to see.'

'Oh,' Lili says.

'I hope you don't mind.' Henry seems confident nobody will mind. 'Unless you've seen it? Most people missed it.'

'I was looking forward to *Dead Poets Society*,' Lili says.

'Not that Robin Williams,' Henry groans with the kind of contempt he had earlier reserved for Woody Allen.

'We watch one film, and one film only,' Lili steps in front of the TV to take a stand. 'It's all we need.'

'I thought you liked *Dead Poets Society*,' Bernadette says accusingly to Dr Freele. 'I had no idea.'

'Oh, I do.' Her eyes are pleading.

'What is this new film?' Lili asks.

'*Wrestling Ernest Hemingway.*'

'Never heard of that one,' Bernadette says. People have spent millions of years learning politeness, Victor ruminates, it would be indecent to throw it all overboard in one night. He takes the DVD from Henry's fat hand.

'Since we're late already,' Bernadette says tersely, 'we might as well have the tea.'

'Tea would be grand,' Henry says heartily. Since Henry has taken a liking to Victor's recliner, Victor is obliged to sit on the piano stool.

Richard Harris is doing push-ups as *Wrestling Ernest Hemingway* opens. Shirley MacLaine, his landlady, comes to the door. He complains about the air conditioner while she complains about Richard being naked. She has a package with a birthday gift from Richard's son, a cheap cap, but coming from his son makes it one of the great caps. All this happens in Florida, where the sun shines relentlessly on old people at a loss for something to do until they die.

Bernadette and Victor and Lili and Dr Freele seem to enjoy the film. Henry has fallen asleep, his head hanging sideways. May he not die in our house, Bernadette eases the cup of tea out of his lap.

Richard Harris was once the youngest ship's captain in the Caribbean. The trouble with that is it doesn't last. In his prime the Harris character wrestled Ernest Hemingway, he tells everyone, though Hemingway himself fails to make an appearance. Harris also married several wives. And was, he freely admits, generally a fabulous fellow. It's no *Ben Hur*, Victor thinks, it's no *Dead Poets Society*.

'Very interesting,' Dr Freele says at the end.

Henry grunts, his energy spent.

'A pleasure to meet you, Henry,' Bernadette says. The others nod and echo the sentiment. Dr Freele leads the way to the white Citroën. Henry waves. He likes us, Lili is thinking, I wonder why. The three return to the parlour.

'We're at a crossroads,' Bernadette says. 'We need to consider the best interests of the Film Society.'

'He's sort of jolly,' Lili admits, 'but I missed Robin Williams.'

'Is it too late?'

'It's never too late.'

By the time *Dead Poets Society* is over, all three are asleep. Afterwards, Victor escorts Lili home through the moonless night.

'You're the only one alive, Lili, who knows I ran in the London marathon. Isn't that a sight?'

'A sight. And I remember it well.'

The Written Word

'There are no heart transplants in the Tarantula Nebula.'

Up to that point he was just an old man blathering, but what he said seemed a mouthful. So I looked at him.

'No liver transplants, either. And, if you ask me, no livers.' He was talking either to himself or to me, there was no one else. He peered into the distance, somehow seeing the Tarantula galaxy, of which, up to that moment, I had never heard.

I'm retired myself. In the late morning, if weather allows, I walk by the rambling river Inny until it reaches the town. I stop to pay my respects at little bridges only local farmers know, the stones blotched piebald with lichen. I exchange a few thoughts with the water below, a leisurely trickle in summer, but impatient in winter and often taking shortcuts across the road. Since I have nothing else to do, I think a lot.

By about noon I get as far as Curly's, an eatery. There are sixteen tables, seating two to as many as eight, all covered in red oilcloth. I sit by the window, the near chair so I can still see the river. I don't need to order any more. The girls know I'll be having a grilled ham-and-cheese sandwich and coffee. In about an hour I am on my way across the square. I walk on the grass; the grass doesn't mind. On my left is the church, a squat structure in dark stone, and atop the spire an iron cross slightly tilting, though nobody agrees with me about this. On my right is a red plastic filling station. People call out greetings as I go and I wave back at them. Waving saves me having to remember their names.

Ours is, in short, an orderly little world and no loony bin. I make a beeline for the green wooden bench facing the fountain. I am a lover of water in its various manifestations and worry that global warming will reduce it all to steam. For years I had the bench to myself, though I always sat on the south end to leave room for others.

Until that day, some years ago, when the stranger was there ahead of me—and on my end of the bench. We exchanged a few words. I intended to leave it at that but he talked on regardless until he made his odd remark about heart transplants.

'You have a point,' I remember saying to him. I had no idea what point he had, but my modest encouragement added fuel to his fire.

'Thank you.' He threw me a glance. 'Diversity must be desirable or there wouldn't be so much of it. But now, tragically, diversity is reaching a dead end.'

'How do you mean?'

'Take fingers and toes,' he said. 'We've had five on each extremity for as long as we can remember.' I nodded solemnly, egging him on. 'Toes in particular have suffered from stagnation since we invented footwear.'

'But fingers have developed, how shall I say, a certain dexterity.'

Now he looked at me foursquare. With a smile, I was convinced, of approval. I figured he was chasing eighty. He had a rugged, outdoor face that sported what I would call a debonair moustache; it was easy to be debonair in our neck of the woods. He wore a shapeless cloth hat of a kind popular in Austria. It covered, I would later learn, a cranium reminiscent of certain Tibetan monks. His eyes were tight together, but that wasn't it; they seemed all alert and circumspect. If any eyes could see the Tarantula Nebula, his could.

'If I had it to do again, I'd assign eight fingers to a hand. Ten if you want, it's up to you.'

There it was again. Some mighty intimation. Sounding off in his understated way as if—yes, and the eyes twinkling as if he were, to say the least, an eccentric. Or, to say it bluntly, a headcase.

'We humans should long ago have developed wings, anyone can see that.' He was wearing a green corduroy suit and already in September, an orange scarf. He didn't look crazy. Average, that's what he looked. 'If birds could make the leap to flight, there's no excuse for us with our bigger brains and know-how.'

'But it's not your… problem.' Later I could think of various ways I should have nailed him, bons mots to tie him in knots. 'I mean, you're not…' Some of the best questions don't need to be asked.

'Yes I am.' He was so quietly sure. Of whatever it was. I glanced around, suddenly suspicious lest some television programme might be pulling my leg. Everything seemed normal, including this odd customer. I felt an urge to be angry with him. But I'm woefully liberal by disposition. He couldn't help himself, I concluded, he just needed to take his medicine.

'And ears,' he said. 'Skin and cartilage higgledy-piggledy and not even efficient after billions of experiments. Do you not care?' It was like the question about beating your wife, only different. I was suddenly tired of his self-possessed hauteur, like a bloody sultan, though I have nothing against sultans.

'I need to be going.' It wasn't a lie. 'My name is Owen,' I added, wanting him to divulge his own.

'Luke,' he said. He held out his hand and I shook it. Five fingers. Of a soft old average hand.

'Luke?' people repeated with blank faces when I made inquiries. In the days that followed I took care to arrive early and reclaim my end of the green bench. Yet I would scan the square, and there was a twinge of loss when he failed to appear. We may have done poorly in the fingers department, but we people are miles ahead when it comes to curiosity. Had I seen that nut case, people would ask, and I would shake my head, until I wondered had I imagined him on a day I myself had forgotten my vitamins.

But after a week or two, when my guard was down, he was there ahead of me, and on the south side of the bench. For a moment I wanted to push the old rascal off. I hoped that, after we exchanged a civilised word or two, he would mind his own business.

'Here's what I'd do if I had it to do again. I'd scrunch all the land together into one big continent.'

'And all the water, I suppose, into one big ocean?' I countered to slow his gallop.

'No islands. Every place contiguous to every place else.'

'No need for boats.' The devil made me do it. 'None of your oil tankers polluting the earth. No need for aircraft carriers and armadas, and forget about your yachts and skiffs and ocean cruises. No Caribbean, for heaven's sake, nor Mediterranean, nor Cape of Good Hope.'

'It's not a game.'

'I'm sorry,' I said. He seemed so hurt.

'No Christopher Columbus,' he then relented and joined my game. 'No Vasco da Gama.'

'So what about the seashore?'

'We keep it. We didn't create all that sand for nothing.'

'We? Who's we?'

'A few molecules one way or the other, a few electrons and other subatomic whatnots here or there in the initial conflagration, and we could have an earth made of iron. Or wool, or sawdust.'

'Or gold?' I opted to humour him.

'Not gold,' he said sourly, not opting to humour me. 'There's truth, for starters. And goodness goes without saying. But beauty is ambiguous. A gold earth would be tawdry and unsuitable. On a golden earth what do you do for flowers, or weeds, or people for that matter? What do you do for acoustics?'

Out of his mind. But then he smiled slyly as if to say, it's only a game. I went home confused. I alerted people—he's back. Provided a few extra details until someone remembered him. Harmless, everyone then agreed. His name is Pepper, or Davis, something like that.

His appearances became more frequent—a week, four days,

then two in a row. Even when I got there first I gave up my end of the bench to him.

'We should abolish the automobile,' he said one noisy day in town.

'How?' Leading questions, I discovered, made his day.

'Petroleum is the culprit.'

'We're back to molecules and electrons, am I right?' I was getting the hang of it. Even in our own town donkeys and carts had succumbed in one generation to a constant stream of cars. However slow the donkeys in the old days, we never had a traffic jam. This must surely be food for thought.

'And chance,' he said. We were becoming friends. 'Never forget Murphy's Law.'

'It would mean a return to beasts of burden: the donkey, the camel, not to mention pigeons. Think of all the hay and potatoes.'

'No need. We'd be strong as horses ourselves if we had exercised the appropriate muscles and mental neurons for the past million years.'

'And speedy as a speeding bullet,' I was enthusiastic.

'As a jet plane,' he amended. 'Creatures of infinite possibility.'

And that was just the physical side. When he thought I was ready, he steered me—I don't know—upwards or inwards to where the molecules were more refined and the considerations more intangible.

'I'd abolish hate.' The pale October sun was too weak to make shadows. The cross on the church steeple cocked its head and paid attention. 'This would call for a radical realignment of all the other emotions.'

'Is there any future for love?'

'We need a new vocabulary. Did you notice there's no word for disinterested love? That's because it so seldom comes up in conversation.'

'Or vice versa.' I wasn't sure what I meant by this. In discussions like ours one threw words in the air and hoped some at least would come down with significance attached. 'What about justice?' I forged ahead. 'What about revenge?' Once one started asking such inflated questions there was no obvious place to stop.

I forget what he answered. At a certain stage words lose their point: either inadequate or superfluous. He had touched my arm. And turned the smouldering eyes on me. For a while that October day I could see through him. No metaphor, this, nor mystical experience. Behind where his head should be obstructing my view, I could see leafless trees. I saw crows on the branches. And behind them Rooney's pub.

Was this a holy fool? In the gritty heroic ages holy fools kept all manner of tribulation at bay. I wondered then whether God, commonly believed to be dead, could rise again. God had a history of surprises.

'I don't even know your name.'

'Pepper.'

At Curly's, next day, the waitress wore a knowing grin, and I could soon see why. Luke Pepper had come in from the cold. Had ensconced himself at what I considered my table. A shiver ran through me. Where I sat now might be decisive. I opted to be gracious and asked if I could join him. He looked different indoors, more fragile. He had removed the hat and his skull shone radiant in the light of a fake Tiffany lamp.

He, in turn, was getting a first good look at me. What he saw was a shorter man, chunky. My demeanour, I suspect, is more solemn than average, the reward for a lifetime of burying the dead. My hair is unusually dark for my age because, when a few gray ones popped up not long ago, I bought a bottle of black stuff at the pharmacy. I have a ruddy complexion and shave once a day, including the area where a moustache would otherwise grow.

'The heavenly bodies,' he got down to business. 'We're only one or two discoveries away from a breakthrough.'

'Hubble,' I enthused. 'Fantastic pictures.' In the narrow confines of Curly's, our conversation grew more discreet. It was insane to think we were alone in the universe, we both agreed.

Astronomical numbers were trotted out, and no matter how vast my numbers, Luke always topped them.

'Will they be like us, then? Little green persons or more of the same?'

'It's more a matter of what we see than what's there.' He was whispering now. 'It makes sense to seek out civilisations at the same stage of development as ourselves. That means they would still be in their bodies. So they would need place-to-place transportation. Food, too.'

'What about reproduction?' Did I mention that I live alone and, frankly, am often lonely?

'I'd search for a planet where there are advanced forms of gratification,' he said, reading my mind. He made it sound easy. And it would be easy if one knew how to go about it—like following directions. I glanced around, but the locals seemed unaware that space-time was knocking at their door.

Luke, for the record, had vegetable soup and brown bread. Outside, I couldn't resist looking up at the infinite sky, and acknowledged it with a surreptitious nod.

He was at my table ahead of me every day, on the chair from which, for years, I enjoyed an exceptional view of the Inny. Our conversations became more ambitious, took aim at more distant stretches of the imagination. There were, among the stars, he would say, happy places. In one lofty digression, he expressed interest in a more user-friendly heaven.

'And a more forgiving hell.' Being a liberal, I have always believed in giving the devil his due.

When he missed a day, I felt bereft. Afterwards, I crossed the square to our bench. A bird had dirtied the south end. Instead of cleaning it, I settled for the clean side. The water had been turned off, exposing the stained stone base and rusty pipes of the fountain. Wild geese flew over, flying high, going away for the winter.

On the third day I grew concerned. Odd couple that we were, I had neither his phone number nor other particulars, but the consensus pointed to a little road I had always thought led nowhere. Too far to walk, I was told, so I set out early. Crows flew uselessly about, tilting in an enviable motion. Luke had the right idea about wings. I regretted never having become part of some radical movement that might have created enough commotion among life's molecules to cause buds to sprout from chosen shoulders until they were airworthy enough to soar. Failing that, I should have contrived some other wild plan to goose the universe, the crazier the better, failure would be more acceptable that way. I would die happy if only I could become one of the world's heroic failures.

By late morning I could see a white house ahead. Since it was the only one, it must be the right one. The crows had abandoned me, probably for personal reasons. It is my custom, when out walking, to speak to birds that come within earshot, and likewise to farm animals. Not that I'm a mystic, but most animals are lonely, even in crowds, anyone can see it. Luke's place was a sprawling structure, a weather vane above the chimney, a once-elegant house turned shabby. A pair of stone eagles looked at me ruefully from crumbling pillars. There was an electric door bell, but I opted for the big brass knocker.

Luke was first a moving shadow behind frosted glass and then the door opened. He wore a loose faded shirt unbuttoned to mid-chest. His face was flushed, as if he might have come from a hot kitchen. A series of emotions, including panic, spread across his face.

'You shouldn't be here.'

'I was concerned.' Behind him in the dark interior of the house I could see nothing but books. There was time for only a glance before he led me outside, pulling the door behind us.

'I hoped you might come,' he contradicted himself. He walked ahead of me back towards the little silver gate between yew trees. Sat on the low wall and I sat beside him. 'If I had it to do again, I'd have met you when we were young.' He said it into space, the way he talked about the Tarantula Nebula. This made me nervous—what could he possibly be seeing? The sun came out, doubtless an accident of clouds and wind currents, but I sensed life was making some statement. Old apple trees survived in an orchard. One tree had fallen years ago, the trunk stretched flat on the ground, yet the branches refused to give up, growing faded yellow apples already raided by blackbirds.

I did not notice the door opening. Now a wraith stood there, white robe to her toes, face spectral, yellow-white hair cascading to her waist.

'Could you come back tomorrow?' He did not wait for an answer, ushered the woman into the house. What the fox said to the little prince kept whispering in my mind all the way home. About how we are to tame one another: just gently come a little closer each day.

Next noon I followed the trail of a high-flying jet out the road. If I had it to do again, I decided, falling for Luke's old gimmick, my knees would not ache nor my heart palpitate. Neither would I be sad. Luke's house would assume a new coat of white paint and then grow grander until it became a fabled city full of energy and interesting people and especially children rushing shouting into the future. I opened the silver gate noisily to alert the population against further surprises.

Luke was wearing the familiar corduroy suit, even the hat. Called me by my name as he ushered me into the claustrophobic interior. Apologised for yesterday's apparition. Led the way down a dim corridor. On the right, pots and pans hung from the ceiling of a small kitchen. Elsewhere, scripts and cardboard boxes and folders were piled on sideboards, precarious and dusty, and stacked solid floor to ceiling. If a storm should blow down the thick stone walls, these other walls of paper would hold up the house. In some metaphysical way they had become the house.

Through open doors I could see other rooms similarly crowded: windows and alcoves stuffed with typescripts and printouts, bound in plastic or cardboard covers—as I would have imagined a publisher's emporium. Could he be? Or a magazine editor? But closed down, surely. Too much dust. More likely an archive. Or a heap of junk.

We came to a bedroom without books or papers. Items of antique furniture were strategically placed. A television set beamed silent pictures from a shelf high on the wall. The ghost lay on a wide brass bed amid gold wallpaper of an earlier era.

'My wife Pamela,' Luke introduced her.

I took her hand, damp and limp, pressed it. She gave me a wan smile. She was high in her seventies, I guessed, but still a beauty. Around her ascetic face her long hair was draped over the pillow, hair that must have been her glory once, must have turned heads. Our audience was over in a minute. I squeezed her hand again and Luke kissed her cheek, but she was asleep. I was the last one on earth to shake her hand. She died the next day.

We were half a dozen at her funeral. As Luke scattered a token shovel of clay on her coffin, lusty singers wearing wings sang in chorus somewhere in the firmament. Or so I sensed—when death visits life, it often opens cracks in reality through which mysteries slip in.

For a week Luke failed to appear in Curly's. One day, after lunch, I walked out the bleak road. Instead of the brass knocker I boldly rang the electric bell to drive grief away.

'I knew you'd come.' He shuffled ahead of me through the maze of paper. 'No one knew she existed.' He threw a glance over his shoulder. 'Oh nothing sinister. Those who knew her had died. She has been eager to do the same for some years. But, being married to me, she was always giving me another few months to get a grip on life. That's why she needed to see you; she always said I could never survive on my own.'

A room with a bay window contained two rocking chairs and a desk on which sat a vintage computer pale brown with dust. From one chair he removed several typescripts bound by rubber bands.

'You'd better explain.' I spread my arms to embrace everything. But he left me and I could hear him in the kitchen before he returned with tea and six lumpy biscuits on a willow-pattern plate.

'The world has grown wobbly, Owen. The Big Bang got us off to a flying start, but look at all that went wrong since then.'

'Like this tea.' I was forever having to bring him down to earth. 'It's abominable tea.'

'Precisely,' he said without a smile. For hours he regaled me about prime matter and ambiguous shadows on the wall of Plato's cave. Mediocre tea, it seems, is only a symptom. More powerful forces need to be addressed. The universe is putting huge energy into expansion but not enough into cultivating a better brain.

'When you consider the primitive mess we came from,' I interrupted him, 'and how long it took to invent the wheel, for example, I'd say the contemporary brain is doing well. Including your own,' I added to humour him. I was out of my depth, having long ago rushed uneducated into the undertaking business. Luke waved my remarks aside.

'All we can do is hold entropy at bay.' Tons of molecules and other notoriously small particles were used up every day. Gone with the wind, he said. Suns, moons and stars were swallowed by black holes. A woman dies and all her knowledge so gradually collected and avidly hoarded is gone. 'When someone made the wheel, it didn't need to do anything, any more than a flower needs to be seen or a linnet heard.' He waxed for hours, as he said, adding words to the world. He made me promise to come back. Since I had no other friends I occasionally wondered whether our relationship was abnormal or typical.

Thereafter I always brought my own tea bag in my hip pocket. Luke adjusted stacks of paper to reveal a fireplace in the room with the bay window. In it he inserted an electric fire boasting two feeble orange elements. Another blow against entropy, I suggested. He smiled good-natured agreement, but I wished he would let himself go and laugh and guffaw until the dust from all those books rose up and went golden and turned the room into delirium.

'The first wheel, the first submarine,' he was useless at small talk and always had a speech ready for me. 'Such things become obsolete. They're lucky if they make it to a museum. If you ask me, only ideas count.'

'Could we stop for tea?' He was, it turned out, a reasonably good baker, and would conjure up a different gastronomical surprise for each visit: bribes, I suppose.

'A phantasmagoria of indifferent ideas roams the world,' he announced after the rhubarb pie. Rocking gently in his battered chair, he would look off into space and make room in the world for all kinds of poppycock: trivial ideas elbowing out profound ones by force of numbers; embarrassing ideas in search of a hearing; risky ideas ditto. He would trot out foreign names such as Bucky Fuller, Albert Camus and a Dane called Kierkegaard.

The universe, he said, was kept in circulation by a small coterie who took the initiative to explore this vast zoo of ideas, rejecting some and polishing others for the world to salute.

'The only humans who fully accept this challenge are writers.' A lifetime of dealing with bereaved people had made me a good listener, a rare species nowadays. I had only to nod encouragement to keep Luke's momentum up.

'The first word—I like to think it was spoken by a woman, though it could as well have been a parrot or a jackdaw. Who may have said *mountain*. Or *toothache*. Or more likely grunted, but with a certain nuance over and above the average grunt.' And he was off to the races. Our discussions, I am convinced, kept him alive that winter. We talked in ever smaller circles until his house full of paper could be ignored no longer.

'I was a doctor. I practiced medicine for a year and a day. I dealt with aches and pains, nothing big like brain surgery. I fell for the usual dilemma: too much pain and too little time. I gave up. I thought, writing. Writing will alert people and then we'll all heal everyone else in a hurry.

'So I became a professional and wrote words morning to night. Raw words and sophisticated ones. See-sawed between past and future—the present always evaporated before I could write it down.' He became eloquent and expansive as if a different lingo were required to talk about writing, until I deflated him.

'Excuse me, now,' I said, 'but are we talking about articles for the paper or big best-selling books that nobody reads?'

'An occasional little magazine would publish an article,' humility descended upon him. 'But no one ever seemed to read it. Eventually I had articles waiting at all the magazines, and novels at all the publishing houses. The rejection slips piled higher, a mountain of rejection. Finally I realised people were not ready. Too busy watching television. Attention spans of shrimps.' Bitterness gripped him for a moment.

'I was ready to go back to doctoring when Pamela walked through the door. She was, in fact, wanting to see a doctor. Until I told her I was a writer. She was a dancer, a ballerina from Vienna, Austria. You can imagine how unlikely it was that a ballerina from Austria would darken my door in the midlands.'

'People are overwhelmed and can't cope with you,' she confirmed his own pessimistic view. 'Yet there exists an audience worthy of you.'

'Anyone who makes such a lavish promise is bound to pay a price.' Silence followed. A grandfather clock ticked time away in the next room. I willed him to be human and fiercely bawl his grief to the heedless countryside. Week by week I could discern him approaching that decisive moment beyond which stretched eternity.

'I wrote to all the agents and editors and told them I was withdrawing my submissions because I had found a new audience. I never heard from one of them. You would think they'd be curious.

'The next day, going over the heads of publishers and other middlemen, I started writing directly for the universe. What are a few pages in a magazine compared to that? What good is a bestseller compared to that? I was surprised other writers had not thought of this before.' He paused to savour the memory of giving the status quo its comeuppance, sipped the lukewarm tea from his blue mug. In return for rhubarb tart, I had agreed to supply him with tea bags.

'It was liberating. No more catering to passing trends. The world was interested—how could it not be? The world had time. The cosmos needed feedback. The cosmos, designed for give and take, is constantly running down unless we give something back. This is especially true of meaning. Everyone knows there is a dearth of meaning in the world.'

'In English, is it?'

'Yes, in English,' he said when he saw my stupid question was well meant. 'Reading has nothing to do with it. And publication, needless to say, is just a gimmick to make money. Only the writing matters.'

'So what did you write?' For months I had walked over and around his neglected heaps of paper without once being tempted to steal a look. 'Articles or what?'

'Articles, yes, if some small point needed to be made. At other times I wrote longer works, some running to several volumes. Forty or fifty novels, it's a while since I counted.' He waved to indicate the whole topsy-turvy house. 'Plays—for a while I thought plays. It depended on the mood of the world. I had only to read the morning paper to see what was needed. Whenever life was going well I'd respond with lyrical poetry. But I must warn you: in a world where people kill each other with such regularity, and galaxies crash into each other on a daily basis, it would be dishonest to write as if life were smooth sailing.'

He married Pamela. Not only was she a great beauty—he said matter-of-factly—'she also had loads of money, a necessary evil in contemporary life.'

'She must have been proud of you.'

'She never read a word I wrote. That time she came looking for a doctor, it was about her eyes. Some rare disease. I would read to her on winter nights, until she informed me the reading was superfluous.' Another silence and a sip of cold tea.

Spring came. I tried to coax him out of the dank house back to Curly's for vegetable soup. He would say he needed to write, but he never wrote.

'When I saw you on that bench, I resisted at first,' he confided one day. 'I was looking for someone young to keep the thing alive longer. That was nonsense, of course. Once the words are written they have made their point.'

I held his hand when demons played with the knocker on the decaying front door. I made him cups of tea, then fed him sips on a spoon. Finally I closed his eyes.

An April shower was nudged aside by the sun on the day of Luke's funeral. The priest turned a blind eye on his heresies and sprinkled the pine box with holy water. The church steeple stood to attention, the cross proud. Since I was the only mourner, the priest suggested I say a few words.

'He never gave up,' was all I could think of saying. And added, 'Goodbye, Luke.' And winked at his soul flying off on swift wings. Lucky old bastard. Everyone knowing him already and greeting him all over the universe, Luke waving back at them and no need to learn their names. Luke's spirit shining in the sun or ducking out of curiosity into black holes to verify his theories. Editors and agents and glossy magazine magnates left out of the loop while the universe thundered that it got his message, agreed with his gist.

The clay was still fresh over Pamela. Soon they would be snug side by side. If molecules were half as smart as Luke always said, this would be a lively graveyard hereafter. Subatomic whatnots would learn their way around, would visit each other in the dead of night, would mingle and multiply and start something new.

If I had it to do again, that's what I'd say.

In his will Luke left me the house, and all the words therein. I walk out once a week and switch on the electric fire to keep decay away. I will live as long as I can, in case anything unexpected should happen.